CEO Wolf Shifter's Surprise Twins

Howls Romance

Aurelia Skye and Kit Tunstall

Published by Amourisa Press, 2024.

Join Kit's Mailing List[1] **to receive notification of new releases and access bonus chapters for your favorite books. You get free books just for signing up. If you prefer to receive notifications for just one, or a few, of Kit's pen names, you'll have the option to select which lists to subscribe to at signup.**

---

1. http://kittunstall.com/newsletter/

Blurb

Her hot boss is the father of her babies. He's also a stranger.
AS DR. MAYA HOLT WALKS into the boardroom, Heath Garrison knows three things. She is his mate. She's pregnant. He's the father. The last should be completely impossible since he's never seen her before in his life. Delving into the mystery, Heath gets to know Maya, a researcher in his company who used an experimental procedure to get pregnant with what she thought was anonymous donor sperm.

Surprise!

A simple clerical error upends their lives, making them soon-to-be coparents. That's complicated by Heath facing Ascension in a few weeks, and the Elders disapproving of him having a human mate. His main focus is on securing the mating bond between them and winning her trust and love, but when Maya learns the truth about shifters, and him, will she run away?

Chapter One

THE MOMENT SHE WALKED into the boardroom, Heath Garrison knew three things. She was his mate. She was pregnant. He was the father. The last in particular should have been completely impossible, since he had never seen her before in his life.

The scent hit Heath like a freight train the moment she stepped into the room. Crisp citrus and honey, with an undercurrent of fertile earth that made his wolf sit up and take notice. His gaze locked onto the newcomer, drinking in her lush curves barely contained by a deep purple sheath dress. Raven tresses framed a heart-shaped face, and those emerald eyes behind cat's-eye frames sparked with intelligence.

Every fiber of his being thrummed with the rightness of her presence, even as his rational mind rebelled. This couldn't be happening. Not now, not with the future of his company hanging in the balance before potential investors. He was the soul of control, unflappable in the boardroom.

Yet she commanded his full attention, her very existence a siren's call he couldn't resist. The subtle sway of her hips as she crossed to the empty seat shot lances of pure craving through his core. When she bent to settle into the chair, the fabric stretched taut across the flare of her hips, and he caught a glimpse of toned thighs. A low growl built in his chest before he ruthlessly stifled it.

Clearing his throat, Heath attempted to tear his gaze away, but her scent caressed him, igniting a primal hunger he hadn't experienced in years. The realization slammed into him with all the subtlety of a sledgehammer. She was pregnant. With his child. The scents didn't lie, not to a wolf of his caliber. They spoke of fertile life, creation, and the unmistakable imprint of his own essence intertwined with hers.

How in the hell was that possible? He hadn't so much as seen this woman before today. A thousand questions ricocheted through his mind even as his wolf rallied, recognizing her as its mate on an elemental level.

"Mr. Garrison?"

The tentative query from his left barely penetrated the haze of disbelief and raw need clouding his senses. He blinked, struggling to regain his equilibrium as all eyes turned toward him, a few furrowed brows in the mix.

Right. The quarterly review. They were waiting on him to kick things off.

With an effort of sheer willpower, Heath dragged his attention from the raven-haired siren and refocused on the matter at hand. "My apologies. Where were we?"

Beside him, his second-in-command and CFO, Olivia Nguyen, shot him a quizzical look before referring to her notes. "We were discussing the latest earnings report and preparing to project growth potential for the upcoming quarter."

"Of course." Heath accepted the folder she passed him, flipping it open to reveal the meticulously prepared financial statements. Numbers and figures jumped out at him, data he'd pored over countless times in preparation for this very meeting.

Yet, try as he might, comprehension eluded him. His mind kept circling back to the newcomer and the baffling realization she carried. Who was she? How could she be pregnant with his offspring when they'd never even met?

Risking another glance across the sleek obsidian table, he found her watching him with open curiosity. For a suspended heartbeat, their gazes collided and held, a frisson of awareness crackling between them like an electric current. Her lips, lush and full, curved in the barest hint of a smile as if she could sense his regard. A flush stained those high cheekbones, lending color to her golden-toned complexion. Her features suggested she had some Pacific Islander in her heritage, and he wanted to trace the contours of her cheekbones.

The urge to simply vault across the table and claim her, to bury his nose against the slender column of her throat and drink in her essence, nearly overwhelmed him. He clenched his fists beneath the table until his blunt nails bit into his palms, grounding himself through the sharp sting of pain.

"Sir?" Olivia's tone sharpened with a hint of rebuke. "If you need a minute..."

"No." The curt response emerged rougher than intended, and he forced himself to moderate his tone. "No, I'm fine. Please continue."

With obvious reluctance, Olivia launched into her projected analysis while Heath struggled to focus on the words. Beside the financial figures, he was jotting a series of disconnected notes.

Who is she? How is this possible? Need to know her name. Scent. Mate? Pregnant?

The meeting stretched into its second hour with no resolution to the burning chaos devouring his concentration. If anything, each passing moment amplified his distraction until he could scarcely track the discussions unfolding around him. He was watching her out of the corners of his eye, studying the elegant lines of her profile, and the swell of her belly visible beneath the fabric.

Pregnant. The thought ignited a fierce protectiveness and a bone-deep sense of possession he couldn't deny. His wolf demanded he sweep her into his arms and spirit her away to his den, to keep her safe and secure until she gave birth to their offspring.

With an abrupt screech of his chair against the glossy marble floor, Heath surged to his feet, oblivious to the startled glances and questioning mutters. "Let's call it a day."

He barely registered Olivia's concerned frown at his abrupt announcement, every step an exercise in restraint. With the meeting finally adjourned, Heath wasted no time seeking out the raven-haired beauty who had so thoroughly upended his world. His wolf prowled restlessly beneath his skin, driven by an inexplicable compulsion to claim her, to pull her into his embrace, and lose himself in her intoxicating scent.

His gaze homed in on her lingering by the floor-to-ceiling windows overlooking the city skyline, one hand cradling the gentle swell of her belly. The sight punched the air from his lungs, desire and disbelief warring within him. This woman carried his child—children, his wolf whispered—yet he didn't even know her name.

Squaring his shoulders, he crossed the room with purposeful strides, his polished oxfords striking the marble with a cadence of subtle clicks. She turned at his approach, those emerald eyes finding his with a mixture of curiosity and trepidation.

"Dr. Holt." The name slipped from his lips, plucked from the recesses of his mind, where he had committed the details of every employee to memory. "Might I have a word?"

One elegant brow arched above the slim frames of her glasses as she studied him with frank appraisal. "Of course, Mr. Garrison."

His name on her lips resonated through him like the toll of a great bell, awakening tremors of awareness that rippled through his very core. The subtle lilt of her voice, rich and honeyed, beckoned to the primitive side of his nature he kept leashed with an iron will.

Gesturing toward the door, he waited for her to precede him, every nerve ending afire with her proximity. The faint scent of her perfume teased his senses, stirring a fierce yearning to bury his nose against her throat and bite her, leaving her with his mating mark.

With measured strides, he guided her through the maze of corridors toward his private office suite. The few staff members they encountered offered respectful nods as they passed, no doubt assuming he intended to discuss some aspect of her research.

If only they knew the truth. This woman, this complete stranger, was his mate. That the child she carried was the heir he longed for, yet never imagined could exist outside the boundaries of his kind.

At last, they reached the sanctuary of his office. He ushered her inside, ensuring the door sealed them away from prying eyes and ears. Only then did he permit himself to fully drink in her presence, to savor the play of her scent across his senses.

"You're pregnant." The words emerged in a low rumble, more growl than speech.

She stilled, her gaze finding his with a hint of wariness. One hand drifted in an unconscious caress over the burgeoning swell of her belly. "Yes..."

A dozen questions burned on his tongue, yet he was struggling to articulate any of them coherently. Instead, he simply closed the distance between them with two strides, entering her personal space until the heated radiance of her body brushed against him like a brand.

Her breath caught, those lush lips parting on a soft exhalation as her pupils flared wide. He could smell the spike of her arousal, heady and intoxicating, mingling with the rich essence of her femininity in a dizzying blend that made his wolf want to howl in triumph.

Reason deserted him in that endless moment. Instinct surged, a primal drive to claim her, to taste her flesh and lose himself in the velvet heat of her body. With one hand cupping the nape of her neck, he angled her face up toward his, their lips a scant breath apart.

"You're mine," he growled the words with a feral edge of possession.

Heath didn't give her a chance to respond before crushing his mouth to hers in a searing, possessive kiss. His hands slid into the silken strands of her hair, angling her head to deepen the embrace as his tongue swept past her parted lips to taste her fully. She tensed for the briefest of moments before melting against him with a soft whimper, her fingers clutching at the lapels of his suit jacket as if to anchor herself.

A low, rumbling growl vibrated in his chest as the rich, honeyed flavor of her essence flooded his senses. She tasted like ambrosia and sin, igniting an inferno of need that blazed through his veins with each heated caress of her tongue against his. His wolf reveled in her surrender, in the way she yielded so sweetly to his dominance, accepting him as her mate on an instinctual level.

For endless, suspended heartbeats, they clung together in that scorching liplock, the world around them fading into insignificance. Only she mattered—the velvet glide of her mouth, the desperate clutch of her fingers, and the rapid staccato of her pulse fluttering wildly beneath his questing touch. He drank her in with an avid hunger, savoring every nuance of flavor and sensation as if committing her to memory.

At last, oxygen became an imperative, and he gentled the devouring onslaught of his kiss. With a final, lingering sweep of his tongue, he reluctantly broke away, drawing in a ragged breath. Her eyes remained closed, those lush lashes fanning across flushed cheeks as she panted softly, swollen lips glistening with the lingering traces of their heated exchange.

Possessiveness swelled in his chest at the sight of her so thoroughly disheveled by his attentions. He couldn't resist brushing the pad of his thumb along the plump curve of her lower lip, thrilling at the way her eyes fluttered open to meet his heated regard.

For a suspended heartbeat, they simply stared at one another, the silence thick with unspoken questions and a dizzying tangle of emotions. Then, like a shattering of glass, awareness flickered in those emerald depths. She jolted back a step, one hand lifting to her kiss-swollen mouth as if to verify what had just transpired between them before that hand fluttered up to push up her glasses back to the bridge of her nose.

"You... I..." Words seemed to fail her as myriad expressions—confusion, desire, and wariness—played across her delicate features in rapid succession.

Reason reasserted itself, and he recognized the precarious edge upon which they balanced. His wolf might have claimed her in that heated moment, but his human side understood the need for explanations, for understanding to bridge the chasm between them and not send her running away.

With an effort of sheer willpower, he forced himself to take a measured step back, increasing the distance separating their bodies. Already, he felt the lack of her like a physical ache, an emptiness that cried out to be filled by her presence alone.

"I'm sorry," he said, striving to moderate his tone into something approaching calm reasoning. "This... situation requires discussion. Explanations."

One elegant brow arched above the frames of her glasses as she studied him with renewed wariness. "You can't just...just kiss me like that and then act like everything is fine."

A faint smile tugged at the corners of his mouth at her indignant response. There was the spark of fire he sensed lurking beneath that controlled exterior, just waiting to be stoked into an inferno.

"You're correct," he said with a slight incline of his head. "I allowed my instincts to overwhelm my rationality for a moment. That was unwise."

And yet, his wolf harbored no regrets, reveling in the way her scent now mingled with his own in the most primal claiming. The beast within him recognized her as his mate, his perfect other half, in a way that transcended mere words or human constructs.

"However, I think it would be prudent for us to continue this discussion in a more controlled environment." With a subtle gesture, he indicated the door leading from his office. "If you'll accompany me?"

She hesitated, uncertainty flickering across her features as her gaze dropped briefly to the swell of her belly. One hand drifted in an unconscious, protective caress, and Heath's chest constricted with a fierce surge of tenderness. His mate, heavy with his offspring ignited a blaze of possessiveness and wonder that he struggled to contain.

"Where are we going?" she asked at last, lifting her chin in a subtle challenge that made his lips twitch with the urge to grin. Clearly, she wasn't one to simply follow without questioning.

"To one of our research laboratories. I have a particular sensitivity to your scent, so there are measures we can take to ensure our conversation remains private and uninterrupted."

Her brows knitted briefly, and she was clearly confused, but after a moment's contemplation, she gave a short nod of acquiescence. "Very well."

Gesturing for her to precede him, Heath fell into step beside her as they made their way through the maze of corridors comprising the central hub of "Garrison Research." The occasional staff member offered a respectful nod or murmur of greeting as they passed, but he paid them little heed, his entire focus centered on the woman at his side.

At last, they reached their destination—a state-of-the-art laboratory dedicated to the exploration of biochemical compounds, and their effects on human physiology. With a coded entry, Heath ushered her inside, ensuring the door sealed them away from prying eyes and ears.

"This way." He guided her toward a bank of stainless steel cabinets lining one wall. With practiced efficiency, he retrieved a small, unassuming canister from one of the secure compartments.

Turning to face her once more, he held up the innocuous container, studying her reaction. "This is a specialized compound designed to temporarily inhibit the production and release of pheromones and hormones that govern scent markers."

One brow arched in silent query, though he detected the faintest hint of wariness flickering across her features. She likely considered him out of his mind, having no idea about the existence of shifters.

"In other words, it will mask your scent from me for a short period of time, allowing us to converse without..." He paused, searching for the appropriate phrasing as heat threatened to steal into his cheeks. "Without the complicating factors of our biochemistry."

Her gaze narrowed fractionally as she studied him, clearly weighing the implications of his words and offer. At last, after a moment's contemplation, she gave a measured nod. "All right. If you believe it's necessary and is safe during pregnancy."

"It is." Keeping his movements slow and deliberate, he crossed the distance separating them once more. This close, her scent enveloped him in another intoxicating wave of citrus and fertile earth, making his wolf rumble with appreciation. With deft motions, he activated the slender canister, filling the air with a faintly clinical mist.

"Just a few spritzes should suffice," he said, carefully directing the vapor to envelop her without overwhelming her senses.

As the compound dispersed, the insistent lure of her presence faded, muting into a mere echo at the periphery of his awareness. The sudden lack of that vibrant connection made him feel adrift and untethered, though he understood the necessity.

When at last the canister fell silent, he recapped it and set it aside before regarding her once more. "There. Now we can speak candidly without..." He allowed the words to trail off, gesturing vaguely between them.

A faint line appeared between her brows as she studied him with renewed intensity. "Without you losing control again?" She was clearly puzzled, but she was also eyeing him with scientific interest she couldn't hide. Her gaze stripped him, and he couldn't decide if she wanted to remove his clothes or dissecting to see what made him tick.

Heat suffused his cheeks, but he met her pointed look with a slight incline of his head. "Precisely."

Those emerald eyes held his gaze for a suspended moment before she gave a slight huff of breath. "Well, then. I believe you owe me some explanations, Mr. Garrison."

Chapter Two

MAYA SHIFTED UNCOMFORTABLY in her seat, her hands instinctively resting on the swell of her pregnant belly. A nervous flutter stirred within her as Heath's piercing hazel eyes fixed upon her, his gaze intense and unreadable. Unsettled by his strange behavior there are many curious as well. Perhaps she should be afraid of him, since he'd kissed her after apparently exchanging two words with her during the tenure she'd had at "Garrison Research," but she certainly hadn't pushed him away."

"Your pregnancy..." His deep voice trailed off, leaving the statement open-ended, an unspoken question lingering in the air.

Anxiety coiled tightly in Maya's chest. Had he somehow discovered her unconventional methods? The experimental procedure she had performed on herself in a desperate bid to conceive? A tremor of trepidation coursed through her as she met his scrutinizing stare. Was she about to lose her job and all her benefits come including the excellent medical care package? That would be a disaster at twenty weeks pregnant.

Drawing a steadying breath, She steeled her resolve. Honesty had always been her policy, and she saw no reason to deviate from that now. With a slight straightening of her shoulders, she parted her lips to confess. "I used an experimental technique." The words tumbled forth, her tone tinged with a hint of defiance, as if daring him to challenge her actions. "On myself."

His brows knitted together, his expression a blend of astonishment and something akin to grudging admiration. She could practically see the cogs turning in his mind as he processed her daring admission.

"An unapproved therapy?" His voice held a note of disbelief, yet there was no mistaking the undercurrent of respect that laced his words. "And it worked?"

She offered a small nod, her fingers idly tracing the curve of her belly. "Yes. After years of struggling with infertility, this was my last hope."

A heavy silence hung between them, charged with unspoken questions and implications. Heath's curiosity clearly bubbled just beneath the surface, his desire to unravel the intricacies of her situation obvious.

Finally, he spoke again, his tone measured yet laced with an undeniable intensity. "Who's the father?"

Hair brow furrowed, taken aback by the personal nature of the inquiry. A flicker of indignation stirred within her, prompting her to regard him with a guarded expression. Yet, as quickly as the defensive instinct had arisen, it dissipated, replaced by a gnawing concern. What if he suspected some impropriety? A potential legal complication that could jeopardize her hard-won achievement?

Swallowing her initial reticence, Maya met his gaze without flinching. "I obtained a sample from the company bank."

A low groan escaped Heath's lips, his fingers pinching the bridge of his nose as if warding off a headache. Without a word, he rose from his seat, his movements fluid and purposeful. "Come with me." His voice left no room for argument.

Curiosity mingled with a hint of trepidation as she followed his lead, her steps slightly hindered by the added weight of her pregnancy. They navigated through the corridors, the air thick with unspoken tensions and unanswered questions.

At last, they arrived at what appeared to be a storage area, the walls lined with rows upon rows of meticulously labeled vials and containers. Maya's gaze swept over the vast collection, her mind whirling with possibilities.

Heath's imposing form seemed to fill the narrow aisle as they walked, his shoulders nearly brushing the shelves on either side. Maya felt small next to his towering height, though his presence beside her now radiated a coiled strength rather than outright intimidation. She sensed a tension thrumming through his body, like a primal energy waiting to be unleashed.

When he glanced down at her, the hazel of his eyes glowed with an inner fire that sent Maya's pulse skittering. She willed herself to meet his gaze, refusing to be cowed.

"In here," he said gruffly, stopping before an unmarked door. As it swung open, Maya drew in a soft gasp. The windowless room was filled wall-to-wall with medical equipment—microscopes, centrifuges, rows of vials and petri dishes meticulously organized on stainless steel shelves. It was a scientist's dream workspace, and she'd had no idea it existed in the building. "What is this?"

"This is the facility we keep all biological samples, but the archival room is separate." Heath crossed his arms, his piercing gaze never leaving Maya. "You want the truth, Maya? The real reason I brought you here?" His voice was a deep rumble that resonated through her core.

Maya lifted her chin, steeling herself even as a thousand possibilities raced through her mind. "Tell me," she whispered. Whatever secrets Heath revealed today, she sensed they would irrevocably change everything.

Her heart thudded against her ribs as he led her through the labyrinthine corridors of the facility. The air carried a sterile scent, mingling with the musk of his presence that seemed to envelop her senses. Each step echoed with a weight that belied the turmoil brewing within her.

At last, they reached their destination. It was a nondescript door with a name plate that read "Roger Beck." Heath pushed it open with a firm hand. Inside, a diminutive man with a shock of fiery red hair sat hunched over a computer terminal, his brow furrowed in concentration.

"Beck." Heath's voice sliced through the stillness, commanding the man's attention. "We need to verify something."

Roger Beck, Maya presumed, startled at the sound, his head whipping up with a look of bewilderment etched across his features. His eyes darted between Heath and Maya, a flicker of apprehension passing over his pallid countenance at seeing the CEO in his office.

"Of course, Mr. Garrison." His words tumbled forth in a rushed cadence, his fingers already flying across the keyboard. "What can I assist with?"

Heath leveled his gaze at the technician, his expression inscrutable. "Pull up the records for Dr. Holt's sample selection."

Maya grimaced at the way he so blatantly stated that, uncomfortable with everyone in the building knowing she'd obtained her sample from company stock.

Beck's Adam's apple bobbed as he swallowed thickly, his movements becoming increasingly flustered. Maya watched, her breath caught in her throat, as a series of files flickered across the screen, lines of data and numbers flashing by in rapid succession.

Finally, Beck halted the scrolling, a single entry highlighted amidst the deluge of information. "Here it is," he said, his voice strained. "Sample 7843A, selected by Dr. Holt on–"

"Wait." Heath's rumbling baritone cut him off, his brows knitting together as he leaned closer to scrutinize the display. "That's the sample I provided."

A heavy silence descended upon the room, thick and suffocating. Maya's gaze darted between the two men, her mind whirling with a thousand unanswered questions. What did Heath mean? What sample had he provided, and for what purpose? She suspected though. How could she not? "Do you maintain a sample of ahem...?"

Heath nodded. "I'm not sure if or when I'll take a mat...get married, so it makes sense to keep a sample on file."

Maya's scowl deepened. "It can't be you. I looked for someone specifically with Pacific Islander heritage to complement my own."

Beck's complexion paled further, his eyes widening in what could only be described as sheer panic. "I... I must have made a mistake," he stammered, his fingers trembling as they hovered over the keyboard. "Let me double-check the records."

With a few frantic keystrokes, a new set of data appeared on the screen. Maya's breath caught in her throat as she studied the information, her eyes drawn to a single, damning line of text—Sample 7843B—Anonymous Donor.

The world seemed to tilt on its axis, a roaring sound filling Maya's ears as the implications of those four simple words crashed over her like a tidal wave. Her knees buckled, and she would have crumpled to the floor had Heath not caught her, his strong arms encircling her waist and drawing her against the solid wall of his chest. She could hardly fathom that her entire world was turned upside down just because Roger Beck couldn't tell the difference between the letter A and the letter B.

"Easy, Maya." His voice rumbled against her ear, laced with a gentleness that contrasted sharply with his imposing physicality. "Breathe."

She gulped in a ragged breath, her mind reeling, struggling to process the revelation that had just been laid bare before her. The father of her children—the twins she carried within her womb—was not some anonymous donor, but the man who now held her in his embrace. The owner of the company. Her freaking boss.

A torrent of emotions swirled within her—shock, confusion, and an undercurrent of something else, something primal and inexplicable that threatened to sweep her away in its undertow. Her hands fisted in the fabric of his shirt, anchoring herself to him as the world spun madly around her.

Through the haze of disbelief, Maya became vaguely aware of Beck's frantic apologies, his voice a distant buzzing in her ears. "I'm so sorry, Mr. Garrison. It was a clerical error, a mix-up in the samples. I should have been more careful..."

Heath's rumbling growl silenced the technician's babbling, his body tense and coiled like a predator poised to strike. Maya Felt the vibrations of his barely restrained fury reverberating through her bones.

"You made a mistake?" His words dripped with a dangerous edge, laced with an undercurrent of something far more feral than mere human anger. "Do you have any idea what you've done?"

Beck shrank back, his eyes wide and fearful, as Heath's imposing presence seemed to loom larger with each passing second. Maya sensed the raw, primal power radiating from the man who held her, a force of nature that both terrified and enthralled her in equal measure.

"I... I didn't mean..." Beck's voice trailed off, his words failing him as he cowered beneath Heath's withering glare.

She tightened her grip on Heath's shirt as her mind whirled with conflicting emotions. The world as she knew it had been irrevocably altered.

And yet, even as the ground seemed to shift beneath her feet, she was clinging to the one constant in this maelstrom of chaos—the solid presence of the man whose very essence had become intertwined with her own, binding them together in a way she could scarcely comprehend.

As the darkness crept in at the edges of her vision, she surrendered to the pull of oblivion, her last coherent thought was it the end of place. She was slightly disgruntled to be pregnant with his child while never having been in his bed.

Chapter Three

MAYA'S EYELIDS FLUTTERED open, the harsh fluorescent lights stinging her eyes. A warm, masculine scent enveloped her senses—earthy, with hints of sandalwood and a crisp, invigorating undertone. Heath's face hovered inches from hers, his hazel eyes brimming with concern.

An urge to press her lips against his surged through her, an instinctive desire to taste him, to lose herself in his embrace. She inched closer, drawn to the alluring curve of his mouth and the rugged lines of his jaw.

Then reality crashed over her like a tidal wave.

This man—this captivating, undeniably attractive stranger—was the father of her unborn children. The pieces fell into place with dizzying clarity. That must be why they had an inexplicable connection. It still didn't explain the pheromone blocker he'd spritzed on her, or his strange behavior, but she wasn't in the right frame of mind two more closely examine his reaction.

Maya recoiled, her cheeks flushing with a mixture of embarrassment and confusion. What had she been thinking, nearly kissing a virtual stranger, no matter how enticing he seemed? After already letting him kiss her senseless once before?

"Easy there." His palm cradled the small of her back as he helped her into a seated position. "You took quite a spill."

She swallowed hard, her throat constricting. In the background, the flustered technician continued his stream of stuttered apologies, his words a meaningless blur. "I...I'm fine," she managed, though her limbs still trembled with disorientation. "Just a bit lightheaded."

His arm encircled her waist, the solid warmth of his embrace both comforting and unsettling. Tension radiated from him, making it clear it took a lot of effort to maintain a respectful distance despite the undeniable pull between them.

"We should get you upstairs," he said, his breath caressing her cheek. "You need some water and a chance to rest."

She nodded mutely, leaning into his strength as he guided her to her feet. Her knees threatened to buckle, but Heath's steadying grip held her upright, his muscular frame a reassuring anchor.

With measured strides, they made their way back through the labyrinth of corridors, the scent of disinfectant and sterile equipment fading into the background. Maya focused on putting one foot in front of the other, on the cadence of their footfalls echoing against the tile.

Yet, no matter how hard she tried, she couldn't ignore the simmering awareness that thrummed through her veins and the heightened sensitivity to Heath's every movement, every breath. It was as if her senses had been dialed to their highest setting, hyper-attuned to the man beside her. Surely it had something to do with the increased sex drive during the second trimester.

They stepped into the elevator, the mirrored walls reflecting their intertwined figures—a striking contrast of his tanned, chiseled features, and her paler, more delicate ones. Maya averted her gaze, suddenly self-conscious under the weight of his intense regard.

The elevator ascended with a soft hum, the silence between them charged with unspoken questions and unvoiced desires. Her fingers twitched with the urge to reach out and trace the sharp angles of his jaw, to lose herself in the depths of those molten hazel eyes.

She clenched her fists, nails biting into her palms as she fought against the irrational yearning. This was madness, an inexplicable compulsion fueled by hormones and pheromones and whatever cosmic forces had conspired to intertwine their lives.

The elevator chimed, and the doors slid open, offering a temporary reprieve from the mounting tension. Heath ushered her into the corridor, his palm a searing brand against the small of her back.

"My office is just down here," he said, his voice a low rumble that reverberated through her very core.

Maya nodded, not likely to have forgotten that, but not able to formulate an intelligent response either. She focused on placing one foot in front of the other, on the rhythmic sway of her hips, and the gentle swell of her belly which was a constant reminder of the precious lives she carried, the innocent souls caught in this mess.

As they approached the door, his hand lingered on the small of her back, the heat of his touch scorching through the thin fabric of her blouse. Her breath hitched as her pulse galloped in her ears. With a subtle shake of his head, he withdrew his hand, and Maya mourned the loss of his contact, her skin tingling with phantom warmth.

He ushered her inside, and she sank gratefully into the plush leather chair, her limbs trembling with a strange amalgam of desire and trepidation. The silence stretched between them, laden with unspoken questions and unvoiced yearnings. Her gaze flickered to Heath, taking in the sharp angles of his features, the intensity simmering in those hazel depths.

Would their children have his bone structure? She hadn't really pictured them yet, but now she found it almost impossible to resist imagining how their features might blend on their children.

She parted her lips, poised to give voice to the maelstrom of emotions swirling within her, but the words died on her tongue. Where could she possibly begin? How could she untangle the intricate web of circumstance that had bound their lives together in such an inexplicable way?

"Have dinner with me." it sounded more like a command, but his expression was gentle.

Maya wanted to go home and put her head under the covers and forget everything that was happening, but it would be churlish to refuse the offer. It was sensible to get to know each other and speak in a public place, where they'd both be compelled to keep emotions tightly reined. "Yes, I think we should do that."

Chapter Four

HEATH GUIDED MAYA TO his sleek, black sports car, opening the passenger door for her with a gentlemanly gesture. As she slid into the buttery leather seat, the scent of her shampoo wafted through the air, momentarily distracting him. He inhaled deeply, savoring the aroma before closing the door and rounding the vehicle. Dammit. The pheromone blocker was starting to wear off.

Once settled behind the wheel, he glanced over at Maya, examining her features. The soft glow of the dashboard lights accentuated the delicate curves of her face, the gentle swell of her lips, and the depth of her emerald eyes. A flutter of desire stirred within him, and he gripped the steering wheel tightly, willing himself to focus.

"I hope you don't mind, but I've made reservations at a little Italian place I frequent," he said, his voice a rich, velvety timbre. "It's quiet, intimate, and the food is exquisite."

Maya's lips curved into a warm smile, and she nodded as her stomach rumbled, bringing a flush of color to her cheeks. "That sounds lovely."

The drive passed in comfortable silence, punctuated by the occasional glance Heath stole in Maya's direction. Her scent, now mingled with the fading effects of the pheromone blockers, tantalized his senses, igniting a primal hunger within him. He fought the urge to pull over and claim her as his mate, reminding himself that patience and understanding were paramount. He spent most of his time in the human world and had to follow the bounds of human propriety even though the wolf inside him was surging to get out.

Upon arriving at the restaurant, he led her inside, his hand hovering at the small of her back, unable to ignore the heat of her body radiating through the thin fabric of her dress. They were promptly shown to a secluded table tucked away in a cozy corner, where the soft glow of candlelight danced across Maya's features.

As they perused the menu, Heath noticed the way Maya's brow furrowed ever so slightly, her lips pursing in concentration. He found the simple gesture endearing, and a wave of tenderness washed over him. "So," he said, setting his menu aside since he already knew what he'd ordered, "Tell me about yourself. What brought you to this point in your life?"

She exhaled a soft sigh. "As you know, I'm a scientist, and my work has always been my primary focus, but I was married, once, to a man named Jerry." A flicker of sadness crossed her features. "He wasn't faithful, and when I couldn't conceive, he sought...companionship elsewhere."

His jaw clenched, a low growl rumbling in his chest at the thought of her pain. "He was a fool to betray someone as remarkable as you."

Color bloomed in her cheeks, and she ducked her head, a shy smile playing at her lips. "Thank you. That's kind of you to say."

As their meals arrived, he made a concentrated effort to focus on light topics. She seemed to do the same, and the conversation flowed effortlessly, punctuated by laughter and the occasional brush of fingers that sent sparks of electricity dancing across his skin. He was captivated by Maya's intellect, her wit, and her obvious pluck.

"And what about you?" she asked, spearing a bite of her pasta. "Have you never found someone special?"

Heath's gaze held hers, his expression growing pensive. "My work has consumed me for many years, and I've never allowed myself the luxury of pursuing a relationship." He paused, his fingers toying with the stem of his wineglass. "I knew I wanted children someday. A legacy. So, I took precautions and stored a sample, just in case. It didn't make sense not to avail myself of the company storage facility, but I might be rethinking that decision now." That made her smile, but despite the words, he couldn't find it in him to regret this turn of events.

Her eyes widened, and she leaned forward, her interest piqued. "Thanks to a couple of questionable decisions on both our parts, here we are."

"Here we are," he echoed, his voice a low rumble.

As their meal ended, he was increasingly aware of Maya's proximity, her scent enveloping him. The pheromone blockers had all but dissipated, leaving him awash in her intoxicating aroma. No one had ever warned him how difficult it would be to control himself upon first scenting his fated mate.

"The blockers are wearing off. I'll need to adjust, to grow accustomed to your scent."

Maya's breath caught, her pupils dilating as she held his stare. "And if you can't?"

A slow, wolfish grin curved Heath's lips as he leaned back in his chair, his gaze locked with Maya's. "Then we might find ourselves in a rather...delicious predicament."

The candlelight flickered across her features, accentuating the alluring curve of her lips. A delicate flush crept up her neck, staining her cheeks with a rosy hue as she held his smoldering stare. "Delicious, you say?" Here voice was a husky murmur, laced with a hint of challenge. "And what, pray tell, would that entail, Mr. Garrison?"

His grin widened, his instincts stirring with predatory intensity. Reaching across the table, he trailed the pad of his thumb along the back of her hand, relishing the silken warmth of her skin. "It would mean surrendering to the undeniable chemistry between us." His voice was a low, seductive rumble, the words caressing her name like a lover's whisper.

Maya's breath hitched, her pupils dilating as she held his heated gaze. With deliberate slowness, she turned her hand, allowing their palms to brush together in a tantalizing caress. "And if I were to surrender, Heath? What then?"

A tremor of desire rippled through Heath's body, his wolf stirring beneath the surface at her bold invitation. He leaned forward, his lips a hairsbreadth from hers, just close enough to taste the sweet, intoxicating essence of her breath. "We'd embark on a journey of exquisite pleasure, where boundaries blur, and inhibitions fade."

Maya's tongue darted out, moistening her lips in a gesture that drew Heath's gaze like a moth to a flame. "You make it sound positively sinful. That's a bold claim."

"There's nothing bold about the claim when it's backed up by experience." He trailed his fingers up the delicate column of her wrist, tracing the thrumming pulse point. "A delectable sin that would leave us both craving more."

A shudder coursed through her body, her eyelids fluttering as she clearly fought to maintain composure. "And what if I were to crave more, even now?" she asked, her emerald eyes sparking with a mixture of desire and defiance.

His nostrils flared, senses overwhelmed by the intoxicating blend of her scent and the heady aroma of her arousal. With a low, rumbling growl, he captured her hand in his, bringing her knuckles to his lips in a searing kiss. "I think you know where that would lead."

Her pulse fluttered wildly beneath his caressing thumb. "And how would we resolve such a quandary?"

Heath's gaze smoldered, his eyes darkening to molten gold as he held her captive with the intensity of his stare. "By surrendering to the primal hunger that simmers between us."

A tremulous sigh escaped her as she swayed ever so slightly toward him, as if drawn by an invisible force. "If I were to give in, Heath? What then?"

With a low, feral growl, he rose from his chair, his movements fluid and predatory as he rounded the table. Cupping Maya's face in his hands, he tilted up her chin, his lips a hairsbreadth from hers. "You'll come so hard, you'll forget your own name."

Hey eyelids fluttered closed, her body trembling with anticipation as she surrendered to the searing heat of his touch. "Show me," she whispered, her voice a breathless entreaty.

A rumbling purr vibrated in Heath's chest as he closed the scant distance between them, capturing Maya's lips in a searing kiss that ignited a conflagration of desire within them both. His tongue delved past the velvet seam of her mouth, tasting, exploring, and claiming her with a primal hunger that threatened to consume them both.

Only the server clearing his throat broke them apart. Without bothering to count the bills, Heath tossed a handful on the table and took her hand in his, leading her out of the restaurant and back to his car. "Tell the GPS your address."

She did so without protest, and the drive back to Maya's apartment was a study in exquisite torture. Her scent filled the confined space of the car, igniting Heath's primal instincts and stoking the flames of his desire. By the time they arrived, he was a coiled spring of tension, his muscles taut with the effort of restraint.

Heath walked Maya to her door, his movements fluid and predatory. As she fumbled with her keys, he stepped closer, breathing in her scent. He'd never smelled anything so decadent before. "Maya." His voice was a velvet caress.

She turned, her eyes wide and luminous, her lips parted in a silent invitation. Heath cupped her face, his thumb tracing the delicate curve of her cheekbone, and then he claimed her mouth in a searing kiss.

Maya melted against him, her fingers tangling in the fabric of his shirt as she returned his ardent embrace. Heath deepened the kiss, his tongue sweeping past her lips to taste the sweet nectar of her mouth.

When they finally parted, breathless and flushed, Maya's eyes shone with a mixture of wonder and desire. "Do you want to come in?" She seemed surprised to hear the question slip from her lips.

He groaned. "More than anything, but I won't. We need to know each other better." His hand dropped to her belly. "We're going to be part of each other's lives from here on out."

"That's remarkable restraint." It was impossible to tell if she was impressed or irritated by that.

"You have no idea." He brushed another light kiss against her nose before pulling back. "Good night, Maya," he whispered, his voice rough with longing.

She pulled back, hand at her swollen lips. "Good night, Heath."

As he turned and strode away, every fiber of his being ached to return, to gather her in his arms and never let go, but their bond had been forged long before they ever met. It was deeper than a clerical error, though he was happy that it had so astronomically been in his favor, that his seed had fertilized his fated mate's eggs, but even if there was no pregnancy, he would have been drawn to her just the same. If he'd run into her before now in the building, she'd already bear his mating mark. He had no doubt about that. For now, he had to nurture this link and make a connection that would only grow stronger with time.

Even though his wolf howled and scratched in his mind, insisting on returning to claim their mate. It was too soon for that, and he'd just have to keep his wolf in check.

Somehow.

IN THE DAYS THAT FOLLOWED, Heath was drawn to Maya over and over. Every stolen glance and every brush of her hand against his ignited a smoldering ember within him. It was a yearning that threatened to consume him whole.

He invited her to dinner again, this time at a cozy bistro nestled in the heart of the city. As they settled into their secluded booth, he was mesmerized by her beauty. "You look breathtaking," he said. His wolf whined in his mind, and he hushed it with a forceful internal rebuke, not wanting to lose control. She wasn't wearing pheromone blocker, and she smelled particularly delicious tonight.

Maya's cheeks flushed, and she ducked her head, a shy smile playing at her lips. "You're too kind."

As the evening progressed, they settled into easy conversation. When he was with her, it was like he'd known her forever. Part of that was the mate-bond, but part of it was just deep compatibility between them.

When their meals arrived, Maya savored each bite, her eyes fluttering closed in blissful appreciation. The simple act of her enjoyment stirred something primal within him, igniting a fierce desire to provide, to nurture, and to ensure her every need was met. He growled low in his throat when her tongue darted out to lick her lips.

"This is divine," she said, her voice a husky whisper. "You have exquisite taste."

He shifted restlessly, his cock suddenly straining against his suit pants. "The true delicacy is the company I keep."

A delicate flush stained her cheeks, and she lifted her glass, taking a sip of water with a shaking hand. She definitely wasn't unaffected. He set out to tease and tempt her, flirting lightly as dinner progressed. She never withdrew or told him to slow down. He could have her at any moment, but he refused to rush this bonding.

As the evening drew to a close, he was increasingly aware of Maya's proximity, her scent enveloping him like a siren's call. He leaned closer, his voice a low, seductive rumble. "Would you care to join me for a stroll through the park? The night air might do us both some good." And cool his libido. He hoped.

Her eyes widened ever so slightly, pupils dilating as she held his smoldering stare. With a breathless nod, she rose from her seat, allowing him to guide her out into the balmy night. When she slipped her hand through his, it made his chest ache.

Central Park was nearby, so he led Maya along a winding path, their footsteps muffled by the soft earth beneath their feet. The air was alive with the symphony of nature—the gentle rustle of leaves, the melodic trilling of birds, and the distant hum of the city, a constant reminder of the vibrant world that lay beyond.

As they strolled, their fingers brushed together, a tantalizing caress that sent tendrils of desire coiling through his body. He fought the urge to gather Maya in his arms, to claim her lips in a searing kiss that would ignite the smoldering embers of their passion.

Instead, he slowed his pace, allowing hey to match his stride. Their shoulders brushed, the heat of her body radiating through the thin fabric of her dress, igniting a primal hunger within him.

She turned to him, her eyes luminous in the soft glow of the moonlight, lips parted in silent invitation. Heath cupped her face, tracing his thumb across the delicate curve of her cheekbone before he claimed her mouth in a searing kiss.

Maya melted against him, her fingers tangling in the fabric of his shirt as she returned his ardent embrace. Heath deepened the kiss, his tongue sweeping past her lips to taste the sweet nectar of her mouth and savor the intoxicating essence of her desire.

When they finally parted, breathless and flushed, her eyes shone with a mixture of wonder and longing. Heath gathered her close, his arms enveloping her in a tender embrace as he nuzzled the curve of her neck, inhaling the heady scent of her skin.

"Maya," he whispered, his voice rough with emotion, "You've bewitched me, body and soul."

A tremulous sigh escaped her parted lips, and she tilted her head, granting him access to the sensitive flesh of her throat. "You've awakened something within me. It's a hunger I've never known. No man has ever Made me want him so much, not even my ex-husband."

Heath's grip tightened, his fingers splaying possessively across the swell of Maya's hip as he pressed a searing kiss to the thundering pulse at her neck. The intoxicating scent of her skin, underlaid with the musky scent of her arousal, filled his nostrils, igniting a primal hunger deep within his core. His wolf stirred, urging him to claim his mate, to mark her as his own.

With a herculean effort, he wrenched himself away, putting distance between them. His chest heaved with each ragged breath, his body trembling with the force of his restraint. Her penetrating gaze searched his face, a silent question lingering in her eyes. She seemed to be asking why he'd stopped.

"There's so much I need to tell you before we become more intimate."

She took a tentative step forward, her hand outstretched, a gesture of comfort and understanding. "So, tell me. I'm here, and I'm listening."

Heath dragged a hand through his hair. He paced, his movements fluid and predatory, as he gathered his thoughts. "My people have certain traditions...expectations that I'm bound to uphold."

Her brow furrowed, a flicker of confusion crossing her delicate features. "Your people?"

Heath nodded, his jaw clenching with the weight of his responsibility. "I'm their leader, in a sense, and with my fortieth birthday approaching, the elders are pressuring me to either ascend to my rightful place or step aside for another."

Maya's eyes widened, a glimmer of understanding dawning in their depths. "And what does that mean for you? For us?"

He crossed the grass in three long strides, gathering her hands in his own to stroke the delicate skin of her wrists. "I have to present you to them, to show them I'm ready to take on the mantle of leadership, with you by my side."

Her pupils widened in bewilderment. "Heath, I... I don't know if I'm ready for that. We've only just found each other, and there's still so much we need to learn about one another." She frowned. "it's not a cult, is it?"

That startled to laugh from him. "No, nothing like that. It's complicated, but I'm hoping to convince you to meet them." He cupped her face in his hands, his forehead resting against hers. "I know it's strange and leap of faith, but I promise, I'll tell you everything soon, but for now, I need you to trust me, to stand with me as I face the elders and secure our future together. Time is short."

She was clearly given it deep thought as her eyes fluttered closed. She leaned into his touch, a shuddering sigh escaping her parted lips. "I do trust you, Heath, and I'll meet your people, but it better not be a cult." Her smile was weak but seemed sincere.

A low, rumbling growl of satisfaction vibrated in Heath's chest, and he claimed her lips in a searing kiss, pouring all his longing hand commitment into the fiery kiss. She melted against him, her fingers tangling in the fabric of his shirt as she returned his passion with equal fervor.

THE EVENING AIR WAS crisp and invigorating as Heath escorted Maya down the bustling city street, his arm draped possessively around her waist. Her scent enveloped him, igniting a primal hunger deep within his core.

As they strolled, he was captivated by the gentle swell of Maya's belly, a constant reminder of the life they had created together. A surge of pride and protectiveness washed over him, and he pulled her closer, his fingers splaying possessively across the curve of her hip.

"You're glowing, my love," he said, his voice a rich, velvety caress against the shell of her ear.

Her cheeks flushed, and she ducked her head, a shy smile playing at her lips. "It's the pregnancy hormones, I'm sure."

He chuckled, a low, rumbling sound that vibrated through his chest. "Nonsense. It's the radiance of motherhood, and it becomes you."

Before she could respond, a voice cut through the din of the crowded street, laced with a mixture of shock and disbelief. It immediately raised his hackles—especially the note of possessiveness underlying the words.

"Maya? Is that you?"

He whipped his head around, his senses immediately on alert as a man approached them, his gait confident, and his expression one of feigned charm. A low growl rumbled in his chest as he caught the man's scent—a cloying blend of expensive cologne and underlying deceit.

"Jerry," said Maya, her body tensing against Heath's side. She gave off unwelcoming vibes and made no effort to hide a grimace, to his amusement.

The man's gaze raked over Maya's form, his eyes widening as he took in the swell of her belly. "You're...you're pregnant?"

She squared her shoulders, her chin lifting in a defiant gesture. "Yes, Jerry, I'm pregnant, and it's none of your concern."

The pathetic excuse of a man's brow furrowed, and he took a step closer, his hand outstretched as if to touch Maya's stomach, which made Heath bare his teeth. "But how? We were trying for so long, and then you just up and left without a word."

Maya snorted. "You said everything when you knocked up your assistant."

The hair on his arms lengthened as the wolf threatened to intrude when he heard that. He shifted his stance, placing himself between Maya and her ex-husband. "I think it's time for you to leave," he said, voice low and menacing.

Jerry's gaze flickered to Heath, his eyes narrowing as he took in the other man's imposing stature and protective stance. "And who the hell are you?"

"Heath Garrison," he said tightly as he fought the urge to bare his teeth in a primal display of dominance. "Maya's mate."

His eyes widened, and he barked out a derisive laugh. "Mate? What kind of new-age bullshit is that?"

Before Heath could respond, his attention returned to Maya, his expression hardening. "Those are my babies. You had no right to keep this from me just because you're being petty about my indiscretion." He curled his lip at Heath before adding with some discomfort, "Amy wasn't really pregnant."

"I don't care about your girlfriend or you." She instinctively cradled her belly as if to shield her unborn children from her ex-husband. "They're not yours. We were divorced before I even knew I was pregnant."

His nostrils flared, and he took a step forward, his hand reaching out to grasp Maya's arm. "Don't be ridiculous. You're just being petty, but those are my children, and I have a right to be part of their lives."

"If you knew how to do math—" She broke off with a gasp as a feral snarl ripped from Heath's throat when Jerry's fingers closed around her wrist.

In a blur of movement, he had the other man pinned against the nearest wall, his forearm pressed against Jerry's windpipe. "Don't you dare touch her," he said with primal fury. "She is mine, and those children are mine. You have no claim over them."

The sniveling weasel's eyes widened, his face flushing as he struggled for breath. "What... what are you?" he wheezed, his hands scrabbling uselessly against his iron grip.

Heath leaned closer, his lips curling back in a feral snarl as he allowed his wolf to bleed into his eyes, knowing they'd turn a molten green with gold flecks. "I'm your worst nightmare if you ever come near my mate again."

With a final shove, he released Jerry, sending him stumbling backwards. The other man's eyes were wild, his carefully cultivated charm shattered in the face of Heath's primal dominance.

"Stay away from us, Jerry," said Maya, her voice trembling slightly, though she appeared strong. "Or you'll have to answer to him."

Jerry's gaze flickered between Heath and Maya, his expression a mask of disbelief and dawning horror. Without another word, he turned and fled, disappearing into the crowd like a coward fleeing the battlefield.

He watched him go, his chest heaving with each ragged breath as he fought to regain control of his wolf. Maya's hand on his arm, a gentle, grounding touch, brought him back to himself, and he turned to face her, his expression contrite. "Forgive me," he rasped, his voice rough with the lingering echoes of his primitive wrath. "I never should have lost control like that."

She shook her head, her eyes shining with appreciation. "You protected me...us, and I'm grateful, though Jerry doesn't scare me."

He gathered her in his arms, cradling her against his chest as he nuzzled the curve of her neck and inhaled the soothing scent of her skin. "I'll always protect you. You and our children are my world, and I'll never let anyone or anything threaten that."

Maya melted against him, her fingers tangling in the fabric of his shirt as she pressed a tender kiss to the thundering pulse at his throat. "I know I should run away screaming when you say things like that after we've only known each other a short time, but it's incredibly sexy."

He growled with hunger, the deep, animalistic kind, at her words. "I want you." He held Maya close, her belly cradled between them, he knew that nothing would ever come between them again.

She mewled softly. "Come back to my place."

He could have lifted her and sprinted to her place in his current state of mind, but he took time to flag down a taxi. When they arrived at her apartment, the lingering adrenaline from his confrontation with Jerry, along with the anticipation of claiming his made, rushed through hi,. He draped his arm was possessively around her waist, his fingers splaying across the gentle swell of her belly in a protective gesture.

As they approached her building, he slowed his stride, his gaze drinking in the delicate curves of her profile, bathed in the soft glow of the streetlights. She was a vision of radiant beauty, her cheeks flushed with desire.

"Maya."

She turned to face him, her lips parting in a silent invitation, and Heath was momentarily entranced by the sight of her—his mate, the mother of his unborn children, the woman who had awakened a primal hunger within him that threatened to consume them both.

"You're sure you're ready for this?" He reached out, his fingers brushing a stray tendril of hair from her face, reveling in the silken caress of her skin against his calloused fingertips.

Maya's eyes widened, her lips parting in a silent gasp before she nodded. "Yes I want to know everything about you, to understand the man...I'm considering giving my heart."

A low, rumbling growl of satisfaction vibrated in Heath's chest, and he gathered Maya into his arms, cradling her against the hard planes of his body as he nuzzled the curve of her neck, inhaling the intoxicating scent of her skin.

"You have no idea how long I've waited to hear those words, my mate," he said, his lips brushing the sensitive shell of her ear. "To be inside you..."

She melted against him, her fingers tangling in the fabric of his shirt as she pressed a tender kiss to the thundering pulse at his throat. "Then take me inside." She pressed her keys into his hands as she said that. "Show me everything you've been keeping hidden, and let me embrace it with you."

A fierce surge of pride and possessiveness washed over Heath, and he tightened his embrace, his fingers splaying across the gentle swell of Maya's belly in a protective caress. This was his family now, and nothing would ever come between them again.

Heath scooped Maya up into his arms, carrying her across the threshold of her apartment as if they were newlyweds on their honeymoon. Her laughter echoed through the empty halls as they ascended the stairs, and his heart swelled with joy at the sound. He would do anything to keep her safe and happy for the rest of their lives.

When they reached Maya's door, he set her down gently, pressing a tender kiss to her forehead as he unlocked the door. As soon as they were inside, he pulled her close again, his lips claiming hers in a searing kiss that left them both breathless.

"I need you," he said, his voice rough with desire. "I've never needed anyone like this before."

Maya smiled up at him, her eyes shining with love and trust. "I'm yours, Heath. Take what you need from me."

He growled softly as he guided her toward the bedroom. His touch was gentle but firm, conveying the depth of his hunger for her. When they reached the bed, he lifted her easily onto the mattress, his fingers deftly unfastening the buttons of her blouse. Her skin was warm and soft beneath his touch, and he couldn't resist leaning in to press a trail of kisses along the smooth column of her neck, savoring the taste of her.

Maya sighed contentedly, her fingers tangling in his hair as she arched into his caresses. "I've never felt so cherished before," she whispered.

"And you always will be." Heath cupped her cheeks in his hand, gazing into her eyes as he spoke. "You're mine, Maya. My mate, my partner, the mother of my children. I'll protect you with my life, and I'll spend every day making sure you know how much I love you."

She seemed overwhelmed for a moment. "You barely know me. If not for me accidentally using your sperm for my insemination..." Biting her lip, she put her hand over his. "It's almost like everything was fated to happen."

His wolf growled in pleasure in his head. She was understanding as best as a human could that she was his fated mate. "We are meant to be together. I knew it from the first moment I saw you." He leaned forward, kissing her lips gently. "You're the most beautiful woman I've ever seen, and I knew that I had to make you mine." He wouldn't be surprised if fate had a hand in guiding the mix-up at the storage facility. How else had his fated mate ended up pregnant with his children before they'd ever met?

Maya blushed at his words, her smile widening. "I'm glad we found each other too," she said softly. "Even if it was a little unconventional."

Heath chuckled, his hands moving to the fastenings of his slacks while she slid off her blouse and stood up to push down the skirt, revealing the sweet curve of her belly. He groaned at the sight, his cock throbbing with need.

"I can't wait to see you even rounder with our children," he said, reaching out to caress her belly reverently. "To know that you're carrying a part of me inside you."

Maya shivered at his touch, her nipples pebbling against the fabric of her bra. "I can't wait to actually have your cock inside me."

He growled, his fingers hooking into the waistband of her panties and tugging them down. He took a step back, drinking in the sight of her naked body. She was perfect, her skin glowing with health and her breasts full and ripe. He wanted to worship every inch of her, to show her just how precious she was to him.

Maya bit her lip, her gaze dropping to his erection as he pushed his pants and boxers down his hips. "You're so big," she whispered, her eyes wide. "I don't know how you'll fit inside me."

Heath smirked, his hand wrapping around his shaft and stroking slowly as he looked at her. "I'll go slowly and make sure you're ready for me. I promise it will be the best sex you've ever had."

She giggled at that. "That's quite a claim, Mr. Garrison."

He grinned, reaching out to cup her breast and tease her nipple through the fabric of her bra. "Just wait until you feel my tongue on you, and then I'll show you what it feels like to have my cock buried inside you."

Maya gasped, arching into his touch as he slipped one strap of her bra down her shoulder. "Please, Heath. I need you."

The desperation in her voice sent a thrill of desire through him, and he quickly removed her bra, tossing it aside before guiding her to lie back on the bed. He knelt between her legs, his hands sliding up her thighs and parting her slick folds.

"So wet already," he murmured, his thumb brushing against her clit. "You're going to be so tight around my cock."

Maya moaned, her hips bucking against his hand as he teased her. "Please don't make me wait any longer. I need to feel you inside me."

Heath obliged, lowering his head toward her pussy and inhaling deeply, savoring the scent of her arousal. He licked his lips, his tongue darting out to taste her, and he groaned with pleasure at the sweetness of her essence. "You taste so good," he said, his voice thick with desire.

Maya whimpered, her fingers tangling in his hair as he lapped at her folds, his tongue teasing her entrance before delving deeper. Her body trembled beneath his ministrations, and he reveled in bringing her such pleasure.

"Oh god, Heath," she cried, her hips rocking against his face as he sucked her clit into his mouth. "I'm so close."

Heath growled, his fingers digging into her thighs as he held her in place, flicking his tongue against her sensitive bud. Her muscles tensed, her body teetering on the edge of release, and he teased her relentlessly, drawing out her pleasure until she finally shattered in his arms.

"Yes," she cried, her back arching off the bed as she came undone. "Just like that."

Heath continued to lick and suck at her pussy, his tongue lapping up her juices as she rode out the waves of her orgasm. When she finally collapsed back onto the bed after a second releasre, panting and spent, he rose to his knees, his cock aching with need.

"Are you ready for me?" At her nod, he groaned softly. He wouldn't have to cover his dick. There'd be no barrier between him and his mate.

Maya spread her legs wider, her eyes dark with desire as she gazed up at him. "Make me yours. Complete the bond." Her voice was husky with need, but she frowned. "I have no idea why I said it like that."

He smothered a grin. She was responding to instinctive cues despite being limited by her human nature. He buries his face in her neck and grasped his shaft, rubbing the tip against her slit.

She moaned, her nails raking across his shoulders as she tried to pull him closer. "Please, Heath. I need you inside me."

He grunted, his control slipping as he thrust his hips forward, burying his cock deep inside her in one smooth stroke. She was so tight and wet, her inner walls gripping him like a vise as he filled her completely. "Fuck." He growled, his fingers digging into her hips as he began to move. "You feel so fucking good." He battled with his wolf not to rut her like a wild animal, wanting to savor this and live up to his promise of the best sex of her life.

She wrapped her legs around his waist, her heels pressing into his ass as she urged him to take her harder and faster. "More," she begged, her breath hot against his ear. "I want all of you."

Heath obliged, increasing the pace of his thrusts as he drove into her, his cock pulsing with the need to claim her. "You're mine. My mate."

She shuddered beneath him, her body trembling with pleasure as he claimed her. "Yes," she cried, her fingers tangling in his hair as she clung to him. "I'm yours, Heath. Always."

He growled, his lips capturing hers in a searing kiss as he lost himself in the sensation of her body. She was his, and nothing would ever come between them. His teeth hovered over her shoulder, on the verge of giving her his mating bite, but he closed his eyes and turned his head, stifling the impulse. Not without her consent and full understanding of what he was, and what it meant to be his mate.

Maya's body tightened around him, her inner walls clenching as she neared her climax. "Come for me," she pleaded, her fingers digging into his back as she arched against him. "I want to feel you come inside me. I need to know you're mine too."

Heath groaned, his cock throbbing with the need to fill her with his seed. "You have no idea how badly I want to mark you as my mate," he said, his voice rough with desire. "To claim you in every way possible."

She gasped, her eyes widening as she stared up at him. "What does that mean?"

He couldn't have a logical conversation while balls-deep in her. Instead, he distracted her—both of them—with a deep, possessive kiss as his hips snapped forward, driving his cock into her with renewed vigor.

She moaned into his mouth, her body quivering as she surrendered to his touch. "Yes, Heath. Just like that. I'm so close."

Heath growled, his hands grasping her hips as he pounded into her, his cock swelling with the need to claim her. "Come for me, Maya. Come for me and let me fill you with my seed."

She cried out, her body shuddering as she reached her peak, her inner walls clamping down around him as she came. Heath's own release followed, his cock erupting inside her as he spilled his seed deep within her womb.

Her nails raked across his back as she writhed beneath him. "Give me everything."

Heath roared, his fingers digging into her skin as he emptied himself into her, his cock twitching and pulsing repeatedly as he filled her with his essence. It was the most intense experience of his life, and nothing would ever compare to this moment, except when he gave her his mating mark for the first time.

He collapsed against her, his chest heaving as he struggled to catch his breath. She was limp and sated in his arms, her body still trembling with the aftershocks of her orgasm.

"You were right," she said with a throaty chuckle. "That was the best sex I've ever had."

Heath pressed a tender kiss to her forehead. "And it will only get better from here."

She smiled, her eyes drifting shut as she snuggled against him. "You can stay if you want." She yawned. "Sorry. I'm so tired. The babies..."

He grinned. "I'm not going anywhere. You're stuck with me now."

She hummed contentedly, her breathing slowing as she drifted off to sleep. Heath watched her for a moment, his heart swelling with love and pride. She was his now, and he would do whatever it took to keep her safe and happy for the rest of their lives.

Chapter Five

THE JOURNEY TO HEATH'S family island had been an adventure in itself. After a short flight to a remote airstrip, they boarded a sleek yacht that cut through the azure waters with ease. As the mainland faded into the distance, Maya was surrounded by an endless expanse of ocean, the salty breeze caressing her face.

The island itself was a verdant paradise, lush with tropical foliage and fringed by pristine white beaches. Heath's ancestral home, a sprawling estate nestled amidst the greenery, exuded a sense of timeless elegance. Yet, despite the warm welcome from Heath's family, Maya felt a subtle undercurrent of distance, as if she were an outsider in this close-knit community.

He took her to meet his grandmother as soon as they were settled into a cabin. As they entered the older woman's humble home, cozy with plaids and flannels, nausea plagued her, leaving her feeling drained and uncomfortable. Heath's concern was obvious, his brow furrowed as he watched her struggle.

"I have just the thing, dear," said his grandmother, disappearing into the kitchen.

Maya was expecting a cup of chamomile or mint tea perhaps, so when Editha approached with a peculiar offering, she had to hide how shocked she was. The elderly woman's kind eyes crinkled as she extended a plate bearing a slab of raw, crimson steak.

"Eat, child," she said, her voice gentle yet insistent. "For the sake of your babies."

Maya's eyes widened, her gaze flickering between the uncooked meat and Editha's expectant expression. A wave of nausea threatened to overwhelm her, but she swallowed hard, forcing a polite smile. "I... I'm not sure I can keep that down," she said, her hand instinctively cradling her swollen belly.

Editha's response was a knowing smile. "Trust me, dear. Your little ones need the nourishment."

Before Maya could further protest, Editha added, "Twins, you know. They'll need extra sustenance."

A flicker of surprise hit her. How could Editha possibly know about the twins? She hadn't shared that information with anyone on the island, and she doubted Heath had revealed they were expecting two yet.

As if sensing her unspoken question, the old woman chuckled softly and retrieved another slab of raw meat from a nearby platter. "Here, have another. You'll need the protein."

"Don't overwhelm her, Gran," said Heath with a hint of warning. "She's only human."

Was it her, or did he give that a peculiar inflection?

Her stomach churned at the sight of the uncooked flesh, her usual aversion to raw meat resurfacing. Yet, as she gazed into Editha's warm, imploring eyes, something deep within her stirred. An instinctive urge to nourish and protect her unborn children overrode her initial revulsion.

Tentatively, she reached for the first steak, her fingers curling around the cool, slick surface. Bringing it to her lips, she took a hesitant bite, bracing herself for the metallic tang of blood. To her surprise, the flavor was rich and savory, igniting her taste buds in a way she had never experienced before. Before she knew it, she had devoured the entire steak, her hunger seemingly insatiable.

Editha beamed with approval, sliding the second slab closer. "Eat, my dear. Your little ones will thank you."

Maya nodded, her earlier reservations melting away as she tore into the second steak with newfound gusto. With each bite, she felt a surge of energy coursing through her veins, her fatigue dissipating like a morning mist as Heath watched with gentle amusement.

As she licked the last traces of juice from her fingers, a contented sigh escaped her lips. Editha's weathered hand came to rest on her shoulder, a gentle squeeze conveying a wealth of unspoken understanding.

"The Garrison men are...robust." Her eyes twinkled with mirth. "Your babies will need plenty of nourishment to grow strong."

Maya's brow furrowed slightly at the comment, confused. She knew logically, diet had little bearing on a baby's size or development unless the mother was severely malnourished. Yet, something about Editha's words resonated within her, as if there were a deeper meaning she couldn't quite grasp.

Before she could voice her thoughts, Editha turned away. "Let me get you some tea, and we can get acquainted while you recharge, dear. Your body knows what it needs."

With a grateful nod, Maya acquiesced, her mind swirling with questions as she leaned against Heath. He seemed unsurprised by his grandmother's offering, and she was too tired to worry about how strange the encounter had been. He'd warned her his family was eccentric. So far, she'd seen no evidence they were a cult, so she'd keep an open mind. And she did feel better, though thinking about having devoured raw meat that way threatened to make her queasy again.

THE MORNING SUN HIT her eyes. Maya stirred, instinctively cradling the swell of her belly as she blinked away the remnants of sleep. A contented sigh escaped her lips as she basked in the tranquility of the moment, savoring the brisk island breeze against her skin. She'd fallen asleep with the window cracked.

A soft knock at the door drew her attention, and she called out a sleepy, "Come in."

The door creaked open, and Heath's familiar silhouette filled the doorway. A tender smile played upon his lips as he took in the sight of her, his eyes alight with heat that suggested he might return to bed to cuddle, and more.

"Good morning, beautiful," he said, crossing the room in a few long strides. He perched on the edge of the bed, his hand coming to rest atop hers, their fingers intertwining.

Maya returned his smile, reveling in the simple intimacy of the moment. "Morning," she said, her voice still husky with sleep.

Heath leaned in, brushing a featherlight kiss against her forehead. "How are you feeling today?"

"Rested." She grinned. "And hungry. I feel like I've been starving since we arrived. Your grandmother's weird steak thing..." She laughed.

A low chuckle rumbled in Heath's chest. "I'm glad to see you eating, but it is a weird quirk of my people. Gran and the others have prepared a feast for you at the pack...main house."

Maya's brow furrowed slightly at the mention of his grandmother, memories of their previous encounter resurfacing. The raw steaks, knowing glances, and cryptic comments had all left her with a lingering sense of unease, as if there were depths to this island and its inhabitants that she had yet to fully comprehend.

Sensing her hesitation, his expression softened. "Is everything all right? Gran didn't scare you, did she?"

She forced a reassuring smile, pushing aside her misgivings for the moment. "Of course not," she replied, her tone light. "Just a little cotton-headed, I guess."

Heath seemed to accept her explanation, his features relaxing once more. "Let's get you fed, then," he said, rising to his feet and extending a hand to her. "The elders are eager to meet you."

She bit her lip at the mention of the elders, her earlier trepidation resurfacing with a vengeance. On the plane and boat ride, Heath had told her something about the island, implying the elders' influence permeated every aspect of life on the island, and yet, she knew little about them beyond their revered status within the community.

Swallowing hard, she placed her hand in Heath's, allowing him to guide her to her feet. "The elders?" she echoed, her voice tinged with uncertainty.

Heath's expression remained serene, his fingers giving her hand a reassuring squeeze. "Don't worry. They won't bite you," he said her, his tone betraying a hint of amusement. "They're a little set in their ways, perhaps, but they mean well."

Maya nodded, forcing a smile as she followed him out of the bedroom and into the sprawling estate. Even from a distance, the air was thick with the aroma of exotic spices and simmering broths, whetting her appetite despite her apprehension.

They made their way through the cabin and out into the village, walking toward the grand manor home she'd seen from the boat. It didn't quite fit with the rest of the small and neat log cabins, especially when she stepped inside and saw the grandeur. Heath led her along confidently, and at last, they reached a spacious dining room, where a long table groaned under the weight of a sumptuous feast. Maya's mouth watered at the sight of the succulent meats and vibrant array of fruits and vegetables, her earlier reservations momentarily forgotten.

There were three figures seated at the head of the table, their weathered faces etched with lines of wisdom and experience. They exuded an aura of authority that was both commanding and unsettling, their piercing gazes seeming to penetrate straight through her.

Heath stepped forward, his hand still entwined with hers as he gestured toward the trio. "Maya, allow me to introduce you to the elders—Samson, Shaw, and Penson."

The three men regarded her with a mixture of curiosity and thinly veiled disdain, their gazes raking over her form in a manner that made her skin prickle with discomfort.

"So, this is the human girl," said Samson, his voice a deep baritone that seemed to reverberate through the very walls.

Shaw's gaze narrowed, his lips curling into a sneer. "Hardly fitting company for our esteemed Alpha."

Maya stiffened, her fingers tightening around Heath's hand as a wave of indignation washed over her despite her confusion about what they meant. She might not understand exactly what they were saying, but it was clearly an insult. She opened her mouth to respond, but Heath beat her to it, his tone sharp and unyielding.

"Mind your tongue, Shaw," he said, his jaw clenched. "Maya is my mate, and she will be treated with respect."

Shaw scoffed, but a pointed glare from Penson silenced him. The eldest of the trio leaned forward, his rheumy eyes fixed on Maya's swollen belly.

"And what of the children?" he rasped, his voice a mere whisper. "Will they be...like us?"

A heavy silence descended upon the room. Maya's heart hammered in her chest, her mind racing as she struggled to understand exactly what he meant. Did he expect her to raise her children here on the island?

Heath broke the silence, his voice firm. "They are my heirs," he said as he wrapped his arm around her waist in a protective embrace. "That's all that matters."

Penson held Heath's gaze for a long moment, his expression inscrutable. Then, with a slight incline of his head, he leaned back in his chair, signaling the end of the discussion.

Maya exhaled a shaky breath, her mind whirling with a maelstrom of emotions. It was clear her presence on the island was not entirely welcomed, and the elders' thinly veiled disdain had struck a chord deep within her. She didn't know why they objected to her, but it was obvious they did.

As she took her seat beside Heath, her appetite had all but vanished, replaced by a gnawing sense of unease. She was an outsider here in a strange world she knew nothing about, and but the fears faded when Heath patted her thigh in a comforting way. He lived in the real world, and she only had to get through a couple of days of his family's weirdness. It didn't matter if they liked her or vice versa. They'd have to endure each other, because she wasn't going anywhere.

For better or worse, their fates were intertwined, bound by the precious lives growing within her, and she would do whatever it took to protect her children—even if it meant defying the elders themselves.

THE EVENING AIR CARRIED a hint of salt, mingling with the smoky aroma of the crackling fire as the group gathered near the beach for a bonfire. Maya wandered through the lush gardens, her steps slowing as she neared the flickering glow emanating from the clearing ahead.

There, silhouetted against the dancing flames, she saw Heath, his broad shoulders tense, his stance radiating an aura of authority. The elders flanked him, their wizened faces etched with stern expressions, their voices rising and falling in a heated exchange.

Maya hesitated, uncertain whether she should intrude upon what seemed to be a private gathering. Yet, her curiosity—and a nagging sense of concern—propelled her forward, footsteps muffled by the soft earth beneath her feet.

As she drew closer, the elders' words became clearer, their tones laced with disapproval and thinly veiled contempt.

"...an abomination, Heath," growled Samson, his eyes narrowed into slits. "You can't seriously entertain the notion of allowing these... half-breeds to inherit the mantle of Alpha."

Shaw nodded in fervent agreement, his lips curled into a sneer. "It goes against everything we stand for and everything our ancestors fought to preserve."

Heath's fists balled at his sides as he clearly struggled to maintain his composure. "My children art abominations," he said harshly, his voice low and dangerous. "They are the future of our pack, and you would do well to show them respect."

Penson raised a gnarled hand, his rheumy gaze fixed upon Heath's face. "We can't allow such a dilution of our bloodline. The consequences would be dire as the balance of our world irreparably shifted."

A ripple of unease coursed through Maya, as she instinctively cupped the swell of her belly. She had known from the moment she set foot on this island that her presence pleasant entirely welcomed, but to hear the elders speak of her children—her precious, unborn babes—with such contempt ignited a protective fire within her.

Before she could step forward and confront them, Heath's shoulders began to tremble, his body contorting as if wracked by an unseen force. A guttural growl rumbled from deep within his chest, his fingers elongating into wicked claws as coarse fur erupted from his skin.

Her eyes widened, breath catching in her throat as she watched Heath's transformation unfold before her. Within moments, a massive wolf stood where he had been, its powerful jaws parted in a snarl that exposed razor-sharp fangs.

The elders recoiled, their expressions a mixture of fear and resignation, as if they had anticipated this very reaction. Samson and Shaw retreated a few paces, their hands raised in a placating gesture, while Penson held his ground, his gaze steady. "Control yourself,

Alpha," he warned, his voice betraying no hint of trepidation, "Lest you prove our concerns justified."

The wolf—Heath—let out a deafening roar, its haunches bunching as if preparing to pounce. She clapped a hand over her mouth to keep from crying, her instincts screaming at her to flee, to seek safety from this primal beast that had emerged from the man she thought she knew.

Even as her mind reeled, her feet remained rooted to the spot, her body paralyzed by a force she couldn't comprehend. It was as if some primal part of her recognized this creature and had somehow always known about the powerful, magnificent beast hidden beneath the skin of the father of her children. Her mate.

The standoff stretched on, the tension in the clearing becoming almost unbearable, until finally, Penson broke the silence.

"Enough," he said as a forceful command. "We'll reconvene on the morrow, when cooler heads prevail." With a curt nod to his fellow elders, he turned and strode away, his footsteps heavy upon the earth. Samson and Shaw followed suit, casting wary glances over their shoulders at the snarling wolf that remained.

Maya's heart thundered against her rib cage while her breaths came in shallow gasps once she was alone with the beast. She should retreat and seek the safety of the estate and the protection of its walls, but something deeper, something primal and instinctive, kept her rooted in place, her eyes locked with the wolf's piercing gaze as his nostrils flared when he turned to look at her.

Slowly, cautiously, she took a step forward, her hand outstretched in a gesture of trust and vulnerability. The wolf's ears flattened against its skull, a low growl rumbling in its throat as a warning.

"Heath," said Maya, her voice barely above a whisper. "It's me, Maya. Your mate."

The wolf stilled, his nostrils flaring as it scented the air, gaze seeming to soften ever so slightly. Maya took another step, her hand trembling as she extended it farther, her palm mere inches from the wolf's muzzle.

Time seemed to slow, the world fading away until all that existed was the two of them, bound by an inexplicable connection that transcended words or reason. The wolf's warm breath caressed her skin, his gaze holding hers with an intensity that pierced her very soul. Then, in a heartbeat, the tension shattered, and the wolf leaned forward, its muzzle nuzzling against her palm in a gesture of trust and acceptance.

A tremulous smile curved her lips as she buried her fingers in the thick fur. She marveled at the raw power and beauty of this magnificent creature. She should have been afraid but had only calm acceptance and a sparkle excitement.

"This is a heck of a revelation, but at least it's not a cult," she said with a small laugh. As heath nuzzled her hand she relaxed against him, feeling not even smidgen fear. She had found her place by Heath's side, come whatever.

As she stood there, basking in the warmth of her mate's presence, peace filled her. The elders' disdain and disapproval faded into insignificance, replaced by a certainty that she and Heath were meant to be together.

No, that was crazy. He was...she didn't know what he was, but she wasn't safe. Neither were her children. Panic rose, and she struggled to breathe. Suddenly, the world around her began to spin, her vision blurring as a wave of dizziness swept over her. The last thing she saw before the darkness claimed her was his eyes set in a wolfish face, wide with concern, as she crumpled to the ground.

Chapter Six

HE WAS ALREADY IN MID-shift before she even hit the ground. Heath lunged forward, wrapping his arms around her to break her fall. Cradling her against his bare chest, since his clothing had shredded during his impromptu shift, he lowered them both to the soft grass, his heart thudding with fear.

"Maya?" His voice cracked with concern as he brushed strands of hair from her face. Her skin had paled and beads of sweat glistened on her brow. He pressed his fingers to her neck, relief flooding him at the steady pulse thrumming beneath her skin.

Scooping her into his arms, he carried Maya toward his grandmother's cabin, the scent of lavender, pine, and sage wafting from the open windows. Editha emerged onto the porch, her eyes widening at the sight before her. "What happened?"

"She saw me shift and fainted." His teeth clenched as he adjusted Maya's weight. "I need to get her inside."

Editha ushered them through the doorway, already pulling back the patchwork quilt on the sofa. "Lay her here."

With infinite gentleness, hey deposited her onto the soft cushions, his palm lingering on her cheek.

Her eyelashes fluttered, and she stirred, blinking up at him with a dazed expression. "Wh-what...?" Her gaze darted around the room, panic flaring in her eyes as she struggled to sit up.

"Easy." Heath placed a steadying hand on her shoulder, his touch light yet firm as he tortured himself by imagining she might suddenly run away from him despite her seeming acceptance during the shock of the moment. "You're safe. I promise."

Her chest heaved with shallow breaths, and her fingers curled into the quilt. "Where am I?"

"My grandmother's cabin." He gestured toward Editha, who approached with a glass of water. "You fainted, but you're all right."

Accepting the water with a trembling hand, she took a tentative sip, her gaze never leaving yes. "The babies..."

He knelt to inhale near her stomach, reassuring himself that the babies still produced a consistent amount of pheromones and nothing that indicated they were in distress. "They're fine." He smoothed a reassuring hand over her rounded belly, his touch reverent. "You just need to take it easy for a bit."

Maya swallowed hard, her gaze flickering to Editha before returning to Heath. "What...what happens now?"

Heath exhaled slowly, steeling himself for the conversation ahead. "You need more protein to nourish the twins. Raw meat would be best."

Her brow furrowed, lips parting in surprise. "Raw meat?"

"It's what they need." He held her gaze, willing her to understand. "They might have a bit more hair than human babies at first, but it falls out quickly, and they won't shift until puberty, if at all with you as their mother."

Maya's fingers tightened around the glass, her knuckles whitening. "Shift?"

Heath nodded, his expression solemn. "Into wolves, like me."

A tremor ran through Maya's body as realization dawned. "I guess maybe I thought I dreamed that when I passed out." She nibbled on her lip for a moment before saying, "You're...not human."

"No." He reached for her hand, relieved when she didn't pull away. "I'm a shifter, Maya, and you're carrying my children."

Her eyes glistened with unshed tears as she searched his face. "Why didn't you tell me?"

"I wanted to, but it's not something easily explained." He gently squeezed her hand. "I'm sorry I kept it from you, but I promise, I won't let any harm come to you or the babies."

Her gaze dropped to their joined hands, tracing her thumb over his knuckles. "What does this mean for us?"

Heath took a steadying breath. "It means...I need you, Maya. As my mate. My wife." He held her widened stare, laying himself bare. "Will you marry me?"

For a heartbeat, she froze, her expression unreadable. Then, as if a switch had flipped, the fear and confusion in her eyes hardened into steely resolve. "No." The word sliced through the air like a blade. "Absolutely not."

Heath recoiled, his stomach plummeting. "Maya, please—"

"Take me home." Her voice trembled with a potent mix of anger and distress. "Right now. I want to leave this place."

Desperation clawed at his throat as he searched her adamant expression. "I know this is a lot, but I swear I'll explain everything. Just give me a chance."

"A chance?" She wrenched her hand from his grasp, her eyes blazing. "You lied to me, at least by omission. You lied about who you are, about *what* you are. How can I trust anything you say?"

Each accusation lanced through him like a physical blow. He opened his mouth, but no words came, his mind reeling.

"I want to go home." She was clearly beyond persuasion as she struggled to her feet, one hand braced protectively over her belly. "Now."

Editha stepped forward, her expression kind but firm. "You should rest, child. The journey won't be easy in your condition this time of night."

Maya shook her head, her jaw set in grim determination. "I don't care. I'm leaving tonight if I have to walk."

Pinching the bridge of his nose, he exhaled a ragged breath. Despite the briefness of their acquaintance, he recognized that stubborn tilt of her chin and the fire in her eyes. There would be no swaying her at the moment. "All right." He raised his palms in surrender, his heart cracking at the wariness in her stance. "Tonight is impossible, but we'll leave first thing in the morning. I'll have everything arranged."

Her shoulders sagged infinitesimally as a flicker of relief crossed her features. Without another word, she turned and strode from the cabin, leaving Heath to face the weight of her rejection. His wolf howled within him, anguished by their mate's dismissal, but he couldn't fault her reaction, not really. He'd kept the truth from her and shattered her trust. For now, all he could do was give her space, pray she would hear him out.

And hope that she might still choose to be his once she recovered from the shock.

The cabin door creaked shut behind Maya, the sound echoing hollowly in yes ears. His chest constricted, each breath a battle as the weight of her rejection bore down on him. The wolf within him snarled, hackles raised at the perceived threat to their bond.

Editha's weathered hand touched his shoulder comfortingly. "Give her time, child. This is a heavy burden to bear."

He swallowed thickly, his gaze fixed on the door through which Maya had disappeared. "She hates me."

"No." Editha's voice held a gentle firmness. "She's afraid. Confused, but she doesn't hate you."

Raking a hand through his tousled hair, he exhaled a shuddering breath. "You didn't see her eyes, Gran. The way she looked at me..." He trailed off, the memory searing him like a brand. It was even worse when contrasted with the temporary acceptance he had seen in her gaze before she'd fainted. It was like that had reset everything, throwing her into a panic she hadn't experienced at first.

"Then show her who you truly are. Let her see the man beneath the wolf."

He shook his head, feeling helpless. "How? She won't even speak to me."

"Actions speak louder than words, my boy." Editha's gaze held a depth of wisdom forged by decades. "Give her space, but don't abandon her. Prove your devotion through your deeds."

Nodding slowly, he allowed his grandmother's soothing advice to sink in. She was right. Pushing Maya now would only drive her farther away. He needed to be patient and let her process this upheaval in her own time.

Stepping away from his grandmother, he crossed to the cabin door, pausing with his hand on the weathered wood. "I need to clear my head."

Understanding flickered in his grandmother's eyes as she inclined her head. "Go. The island will soothe your spirit."

With a final glance over his shoulder, he slipped outside, the cool evening air caressing his face. Inhaling deeply, he let the rich scents of pine and earth fill his lungs, grounding him in the primal essence of the island.

His bare feet crunched over the packed dirt path leading away from the cabin, the trees closing in around him like sentinels. With each step, the tension coiled within him loosened infinitesimally, the weight on his shoulders lightening.

Reaching a secluded clearing, Heath paused, tilting his head back to gaze at the canopy of stars winking overhead. The tranquility of the island seeped into his bones, the night breeze whispering over his bare skin. Closing his eyes, he focused inward, attuning himself to the primal energy thrumming through his veins.

The change rippled through him, starting as a tingle at the base of his spine before blossoming outward in a wave of delicious heat. Bones shifted and reformed, muscles elongating as dark fur sprouted over his skin. When the transformation completed, he opened his eyes, the world taking on a sharper clarity through his lupine senses. Scents and sounds bombarded him, each one vivid and distinct.

With a powerful surge of his haunches, he launched himself into a loping run, his paws devouring the ground. The wind whipped through his fur as he wove between the trees, his wolf reveling in the freedom of the hunt.

A tremor in the underbrush caught his attention, his ears swiveling toward the telltale rustle. Slowing to a prowl, he dropped into a crouch, every muscle coiled with predatory grace. A flash of movement betrayed the presence of a plump rabbit, its nose twitching as it nibbled on a patch of clover. Heath's jaws parted, his tongue lolling as he tasted the creature's scent on the air.

Bunching his powerful hindquarters, he sprang forward in a blur of fur and muscle. The rabbit startled, darting away in a frantic zigzag, but Heath was faster, his jaws snapping shut around its trembling body with a decisive crunch.

Warmth flooded his muzzle as the rabbit's lifeblood spilled over his tongue. He swallowed the first few mouthfuls greedily, the rich flavor igniting his primal instincts. As he consumed his kill, images flickered through his mind—Maya's face contorted with anger and fear, her eyes glistening with unshed tears. A low whine escaped his throat, the memory lancing through him like a physical pain.

He had hurt her, shattering the fragile trust between them with his deception. The wolf raged against her rejection, yearning to claim her as his mate, his other half, but the man had to maintain control. Approaching her now, especially in this state, would only frighten her more.

The man in him understood her turmoil, her need for space to process this shocking revelation. He would give her that time, no matter how excruciating the wait.

Licking the last traces of blood from his muzzle, he rose to his feet, his belly sated for the moment. With a shake of his powerful shoulders, he turned and loped deeper into the forest, allowing the primal rhythms of the island to soothe his troubled spirit.

The scents and sounds enveloped him, each one vivid and distinct—the earthy tang of decaying leaves, the distant call of a night bird, the whisper of wind through the branches overhead. He lost himself in the sensations, letting them wash over him in a calming tide.

As the miles fell away beneath his paws, the knot of tension within him slowly unraveled. His mind cleared, the anguish of Maya's rejection fading to a dull ache in his chest.

He knew their bond could never be truly severed, not when their essences were so deeply intertwined. She carried his children within her womb. That sacred connection bound them together, no matter how much she might rail against it now.

A flicker of hope kindled in his heart as he ran, fueled by the steadfast belief she would come around in time. Maya was strong. Once the shock wore off, and she had processed this new reality, she would see the truth.

That they were meant to be mates and were partners bound by an unbreakable tie.

He would wait, however long it took, to prove himself worthy of her trust and love. He would lay himself bare, holding nothing back, until she saw him for who and what he truly was.

A low, rumbling howl tore from his throat, echoing through the trees in a primal affirmation. He was Heath Garrison, Alpha and protector, and he would fight for his mate, his family, with every ounce of his being. The hunt was far from over. He had merely been given a new prey to track—the heart of the woman he loved.

Chapter Seven

SHE WAS ALREADY AWAKE when the light changed to signal the arrival of morning. It had been impossible to get much sleep last night. She'd woken with a nightmare of being stalked by Heath's wolf and hadn't fallen back to sleep since then. With the light, she stirred, her hand instinctively resting on the swell of her belly, feeling the gentle movements of her unborn twins. Unease crept over her as she remembered their plans to leave the island today.

Pushing back the covers, Maya slipped out of bed and padded across the room, drawn to the window. The lush greenery of the island stretched out before her, but something felt amiss. Her gaze swept the shoreline, searching for the boat that was supposed to ferry them back to the mainland, but it was nowhere to be seen.

A knot formed in her stomach as suspicion took root. Were they conspiring to keep her here? The thought sent a shiver down her spine. She wrapped her arms around herself, trying to quell the rising panic.

The door opened behind her, and Heath's familiar presence filled the room. "The boat's gone."

She whirled around, her eyes wide with alarm. "What do you mean, gone?"

Heath's jaw tightened, his expression grim. "It's missing. Someone has taken it."

Her heart raced as the implications sank in. They were trapped on this island with people she barely knew, who were something not human. A cold sweat broke out on her skin as fear gripped her. "They're going to steal my babies."

Heath closed the distance between them, his hands settling on her shoulders in a reassuring gesture. "No one is going to steal our children, Maya." His voice was low, steady, an anchor in the storm of her emotions.

She searched his eyes, desperate for the truth. She wanted to sink into him, but fear held her back. "Then why? Why would they do this?"

A muscle twitched in his jaw as he considered his words carefully. "Someone is conspiring to keep us here, that much is clear, but it's not about taking the babies." He paused, his gaze holding hers. "They want me to take over Alpha, and I guess they're willing to accept you as Lupina."

"What?"

"The female Alpha of the pack."

Maya recoiled, shaking her head vehemently. "That's crazy. I'm human. They don't want me, and I don't want to be here."

His expression softened, and he cupped her face in his calloused hands, the warmth of his touch sending a shiver through her despite her lingering fear. "You're wrong. They see you as the better option for Lupina than my cousin, since I'd still be Alpha that way."

Maya's brow furrowed, confused. Her lips parted, but no words came out as she struggled to comprehend what he meant. "You're going to have to explain that."

Heath's thumb traced the curve of her cheekbone until she turned her head from him, eliciting a small sigh. He seemed pained by her withdrawal. "Tamsin is more than qualified to lead the pack, and she's been acting as Beta while I've been in the city, overseeing things in my absence." A flicker of regret passed across his features. "The elders are old-fashioned. They'd rather have a human Lupina with a strong male Alpha than a female Alpha."

Maya's breath caught as she shook her head. A human Lupina? The concept seemed absurd, a contradiction in terms. How could a human be an Alpha over wolves?

God, this place was making her insane. She was honestly pondering these concepts. Still, how could she pretend she hadn't seen Heath shift last night? She shook her head slowly, her gaze searching his face for any hint of deception or jest but found only sincerity etched in the lines of his rugged features.

"But... how?" The question slipped past her lips, a whisper barely audible. "I'm not one of you. I'm just a regular human." She glared at him, taking a step back. "I have zero interest in becoming a werewolf, or whatever, so don't even think about it."

Heath's hands slid down to her shoulders, his touch grounding her in the moment. "You're carrying my children. That alone makes you extraordinary in their eyes." A hint of a smile tugged at the corners of his mouth. "To reassure you, I can't make you a shifter anyway. You're born with the gene. It's just a different evolutionary path."

"Oh." That was a relief. "But the elders..." she began, her voice trailing off as uncertainty crept in.

Heath's expression hardened, a flicker of frustration passing across his features. "The elders are stuck in their ways, clinging to outdated traditions and prejudices." His fingers tightened on her shoulders, his gaze intense. "They're reluctant to accept you, but they'll have to see you as the solution to their dilemma—a way to avoid having a female Alpha while still maintaining the bloodline once I ascend to Alpha."

Maya's mouth was dry. They wanted her to be their female figurehead, simply because she was carrying Heath's children even though she wasn't a shifter herself. The notion was ridiculous. "I don't know the first thing about being a pack leader, Heath," she said with desperation. "I'm just a scientist, a researcher. I'm not cut out for this."

"You underestimate yourself. You have the strength within you, but they aren't expecting a leader. They want you to be my loving partner and keep to yourself." He grimaced. "I'm not okay with that. I want you to be happy and confident in whatever your role. We're in this together, remember?"

A lump formed in her throat. She searched his gaze, seeking the truth in his words, and found a depth of conviction that both awed and terrified her. "You won't hurt me, will you?" It was more a statement than a question.

He looked wounded before his expression became neutral. "Never. We don't harm humans unless it's in self-defense, and I'd never harm my mate and the mother of my children. Even if you never accept the bond, I'll watch over you until its severance drives me insane."

"What?"

He grimaced. "I'm not trying to manipulate you, but if a mate doesn't accept the bond, most wolves go mad from the rejection. We tend to wander into the wilderness and lose ourselves in our wolf-form until nothing of the human remains. It's the only way to deal with the pain."

She scowled. "That's not fair to you or me. Who came up with that idea?"

He gave a small smile. "Blame evolution. I don't know. I'll never force you to do anything you want, and I'm working on getting us off the island. Back in the city, you can choose your own path. If I lose myself, I'll still ensure our children are well-provided for after I'm gone."

His words were so matter-of-fact, as though he felt nothing, but she saw the fear and hint of panic in his gaze. She didn't believe he was lying to manipulate her when she saw how deeply concerned he was about the possibility of her refusing him.

She sighed. "I don't know how I feel. I'm scared, but I guess not of you. You're my only defense here, so were in this together for now, I guess." Slowly, she nodded, her hands coming to rest on his forearms, anchoring herself to his solid presence.

Heath's lips curved into a soft smile, and he leaned in, pressing a tender kiss to her forehead. "I won't let them force you into anything you don't want." His voice was a low rumble, resonating with a protective fierceness that sent a shiver down her spine. "I won't let anyone harm you or our children."

Maya nodded, her fingers curling into the fabric of his shirt as she clung to him. For now, she would have to trust him and trust in the bond that had inexplicably formed between them. Perhaps she might be able to eventually trust this group who was more than human. "I'd like to meet Tamsin." She notched up her chin. "I want to get her opinion on all this since it clearly affects her."

Heath studied her for a moment before giving a curt nod. "Very well." His deep voice rumbled with a hint of reluctance. "If you're certain."

She lifted her chin, meeting his gaze with unwavering determination. "I am. If it's safe, I mean."

A muscle twitched in Heath's jaw, but he just said, "No one here will hurt you physically, but they might hurt your feelings." He turned on his heel and strode toward the door, his movements fluid and purposeful.

Maya followed, her steps a little less confident as a flicker of doubt crept into her mind. What was she doing, insisting on meeting this Tamsin? The woman who should be the one leading these people, not a human outsider like herself. A shiver ran down Maya's spine as she contemplated the potential consequences of her request.

They left the guest cabin, and she inhaled the scent of pine and sunshine, finding it soothing in spite of the fears this place also inspired. Heath's footsteps echoed on the ground, each step carrying him farther away from her. Maya quickened her pace, her hands resting on the sides of her belly as she struggled to keep up with his long strides.

They descended a winding staircase carved into the side of the mountain, and the air grew cooler and more humid with each step. The scent of damp earth and moss filled Maya's nostrils, mingling with the faint aroma of wood smoke. It was a primal scent that stirred something deep within her, a connection to the wild that she couldn't quite explain.

There was a large cabin surrounded by a vertical log fence at the bottom of the stairs, and a heavy wooden door loomed before them. Heath paused, his hand resting on the iron handle as he glanced back at Maya. A silent question lingered in his eyes, giving her one last chance to reconsider.

She swallowed hard, her heart pounding in her chest, but she gave a resolute nod. There was no turning back now. With a creak of hinges, Heath pushed open the door, and they stepped out into a lush, verdant courtyard enclosed by the upright logs. The cabin was easier to see here, and she admired how smoothly it was put together.

The air was thick with the scent of blooming flowers and damp earth. A woman stood with her back to them in the center of the courtyard, clad in a simple tunic that clung to her curves. It resembled the garb Maya had seen others on the island wearing. It was probably easy to remove when they had need to shift. Long, chestnut hair cascaded down her back in frizzy waves, swaying with each graceful movement.

As if sensing their presence, she turned, and she gasped. Tamsin's features were striking, her high cheekbones and full lips framing eyes that shone with an intelligence that bordered on predatory. There was a feral grace to her movements, a raw power simmering just beneath the surface.

Those piercing eyes locked onto Maya, and a shiver run down her spine, as if she were being assessed, weighed, and measured by this woman who seemed so at home in this wild place.

"Tamsin." Heath's voice broke the tense silence, drawing the woman's gaze away from her. "This is Maya Holt."

Tamsin's full lips curved into a smile that didn't quite reach her eyes. "The human Lupina." Her voice was rich and melodic, laced with a hint of amusement. "You have a hard sell to the elders, cousin."

She bristled at the subtle mockery in Tamsin's tone, her chin lifting defiantly. "I'm not your Lupina and don't want to be."

A low chuckle rumbled from Tamsin's throat, and she took a step closer before Maya had even blinked. "Not yet, perhaps, but you carry the future of our pack within you." Her gaze flickered to Maya's swollen belly, and a flicker of something akin to envy passed across her features.

She put a hand over her belly in a protective gesture that didn't go unnoticed by Tamsin. The other woman's lips quirked into a knowing smile, and she held up her hands in a placating gesture.

"Peace, Maya. I mean you no harm." Her voice was soothing, but there was an undercurrent of steel beneath the words. "I merely wish to understand your place in all of this, since you'll be supplanting me."

Maya's gaze darted to Heath, seeking reassurance, but his expression was unreadable, a mask of stoic neutrality. She swallowed hard, forcing herself to meet Tamsin's piercing stare.

"I don't know what my place is," she said, her voice wavering slightly. "I'm just a scientist, and I never asked for any of this. I don't want to take your place, and I sure don't want to stay on the island."

Tamsin's brow arched, and she took another step closer, her movements slow and deliberate, but her gaze was no less intense. "And yet, here you are, carrying the heirs to our pack." Her gaze flickered to Heath, a silent question passing between them.

His jaw tightened, and he shifted his stance, subtly positioning himself between Maya and Tamsin. "She's more than just a vessel. Maya is my mate."

A flicker of surprise crossed Tamsin's features, quickly masked by a neutral expression. "Is that so?" Her gaze returned to Maya, assessing her with a new intensity. "Then perhaps there is more to you than meets the eye."

Despite his cousin's assurance she wasn't going to harm her, Maya's palms grew damp with nervous sweat. She opened her mouth to respond, but the words caught in her throat, strangled by a sudden wave of uncertainty.

Tamsin seemed to sense her hesitation, and her expression softened ever so slightly. "Whatever happens, I hold no ill will toward you." She looked at Heath next. "Not much toward you."

To her surprise, he laughed. "I'm sorry you've gotten comfortable as the Alpha, and now I'm back."

Tamsin shrugged. "The question is, do you really want to be the Alpha?" Before he could reply, Tamsin turned toward the cabin, disappearing into the shadows of the courtyard before entering her home and closing the door with finality.

She looked at Heath. "Do you want to be Alpha?"

He didn't hesitate. "No, but I'm not sure if I can get out of it." He walked closer, holding out a hand. "Will you walk with me and see more of this place?"

She rested her palm against his, no longer frightened of Heath. At the moment, she was worried about him. He seemed so lost that it was all she could do not to throw herself into his arms and assure him she would be with him. Part of her was sure she'd already decided that, but the other part of her, ruled by logic and reason, didn't see how she could accept being mated to a creature that seemed more magic than man, despite his talk of evolution.

Chapter Eight

AS THEY WALKED, HEATH pointed out various flora and fauna, sharing his knowledge of the island's natural wonders. Maya's initial hesitation gradually dissipated as she marveled at the vibrant colors and intricate patterns adorning the exotic plants.

"This place is breathtaking," she said, her fingers tracing the delicate petals of a crimson flower. "It's like a hidden paradise." One that hid unbelievable secrets.

His chest swelled with pride at her appreciation for the island's beauty. "I'm glad you find it captivating. This is merely a glimpse of what the island has to offer. I love parts of it, but the city..." He shrugged. "I'm happy there."

As they continued their stroll, the chirping birds accompanied their footsteps. Maya paused, closing her eyes and inhaling deeply to savor the rich, earthy scents that permeated the air. A gentle breeze caressed her face, carrying the faint aroma of the ocean.

"It's so peaceful here."

He nodded, his gaze locked on hers when she opened her eyes. "The island has a way of calming the soul, if one allows it."

For the rest of the day, Heath introduced Maya to various members of the pack, each encounter serving as a window into the intricate dynamics and customs of their community. Some greeted her with warmth and curiosity, while others maintained a guarded distance, their skepticism evident. None claimed to have any knowledge of the missing boat.

Late that afternoon, they stumbled on a group of children engaged in a spirited game, their laughter echoing through the clearing. Maya watched, entranced, as the youngsters shifted effortlessly between their human and wolf forms, their innocent joy infectious.

"They're so carefree," she whispered, her hand instinctively resting on her swollen belly. Would her babies be able to do that? Part of her hoped fervently that the couldn't, while another part marveled at the unusual heritage of her children.

Heath's expression softened as he observed the scene. "They're the embodiment of our pack's future, a future that our children will be a part of even if they're in the city and never meet their cousins and packmates."

Maya's gaze met his. "And what of you? You speak of the place with love and reverence, but do you envision yourself as the pack's leader? You said no earlier, but I wonder if you're being honest with yourself."

Heath paused as though carefully considering his response. "My priorities have shifted. While the role of Alpha holds significance, my focus lies with you and our children. Ensuring your well-being and happiness is paramount."

Maya searched his face, sensing the sincerity in his words. A small smile tugged at the corners of her lips as she nodded, her fingers intertwining with his.

As the day progressed, her initial trepidation gradually gave way to a sense of wonder and acceptance. She marveled at the close-knit bonds that existed within the pack and the support they offered one another. Despite that, she noticed the occasional undercurrent of tension that rippled through the community.

During an evening walk along the beach, the rhythmic crashing of waves providing a soothing backdrop, Maya broached the subject that had been weighing on her mind. "I sense a certain...resistance from some members of the pack. They're nice enough, but they don't want me among them, and I don't think I can be happy living here."

Heath's jaw tightened imperceptibly, his gaze fixed on the horizon. "There are those who cling to tradition, who view our union as a deviation from the established norms, and they would likely make you more unhappy."

Her brow furrowed as she processed his words. "How do you view our situation?"

He turned to face her, his eyes shimmering with a depth of emotion that rendered her breathless. "I view it as a profound blessing and a chance to forge a new path that embraces the best of both worlds."

Her lips curved into a tender smile as she leaned into his embrace, her head resting against his chest. Surrounded by the tranquility of the island, and her mate, she felt a sense of belonging, a connection that transcended the physical realm.

He felt that same connection, but it was apparent his heart yearned for something beyond the confines of the island. While he cherished the sanctuary it provided, she sensed his restlessness at being confined there without the boat. How would he endure living his life there if he became Alpha?

"You're restless in spite of the peacefulness of this place."

He met her gaze, his expression one of contemplation. He remained silent for a moment, gathering his thoughts before responding. "You're perceptive. While this island holds a special place in my heart, the idea of permanently residing here as the Alpha doesn't suit me. I've been putting off making the decision, but my Ascension looms, and it's time to decide if I'm staying or going."

"Do you know yet?"

Instead of answering, he leaned in, capturing her lips in a searing kiss. The contact sent a jolt of electricity through her body, igniting a fire that threatened to consume her. She sighed when he deepened the kiss, his tongue plunging into her mouth.

She plunged her fingers into his hair, tangling in the dark strands as she pulled him closer. His hands roamed her body, exploring the curves and planes. With a growl, he swept her into his arms, carrying her from the beach and back to their cabin seemingly without effort. He strode inside, kicking the door shut behind them before he laid her on the bed.

His eyes glowed with desire as he gazed down at her. "You're so beautiful."

Maya blushed, her heart pounding as he slowly removed his clothing. She couldn't tear her gaze away from his muscular form, her eyes lingering on his impressive erection. She bit her lip, anticipation coiling in her belly as he joined her on the bed.

Heath kissed her again, his lips trailing down her neck and along her collarbone. She gasped as he cupped her breasts, his thumbs brushing over her nipples through the fabric of her dress. She arched into his touch, her body aching for more.

He growled, his fingers deftly unfastening the buttons on her dress. He pushed the fabric aside, exposing her bare skin to his hungry gaze. "You're so perfect." He bent his head, his lips hovering near her nipple. "You'll feed our children someday, but first, I'll please you."

Maya moaned as he sucked her nipple into his mouth, his tongue swirling around the sensitive bud. Her hands clutched at his shoulders, her nails digging into his skin as he teased her. He moved to her other breast, lavishing it with the same attention before continuing his exploration of her body.

His lips trailed down her swollen stomach, his tongue dipping into her navel before moving lower. He paused to cup her stomach, smiling when one of the twins kicked him. "They're strong."

"Like their father," she said, her voice husky with desire.

His eyes flashed with amusement. "I hope they inherit your beauty."

Maya blushed, her cheeks heating at the compliment. "I'm sure they will."

Heath chuckled, his hands sliding up her thighs and parting her legs. "You're so wet for me already." He licked his lips, his fingers tracing her slick folds. "I can't wait to taste you."

Maya gasped as he lowered his head, his tongue darting out to flick against her clit. He teased her, his fingers slipping inside her as he lapped at her pussy. She moaned, her hips bucking against his face as he brought her to the brink of release. "Please, Heath. Don't stop."

He growled, his fingers curling inside her as he sucked her clit into his mouth. She cried out, shuddering as she came. He continued to lick and suck at her clit, drawing out her pleasure until she was writhing beneath him.

"You taste so good," he murmured, his voice thick with desire. "I could spend all night between your legs."

Maya whimpered, her body trembling as he continued to tease her. "I need you inside me," she pleaded, her fingers tangling in his hair as she tried to pull him closer. "I want your cock stretching me."

Heath groaned, his eyes flashing with lust as he rose to his knees. "I'll give you what you need."

Maya gasped as he gripped her hips, flipping her onto her hands and knees. He positioned her on the edge of the bed, his hands caressing her ass before he spread her legs wide. She moaned as he rubbed the tip of his cock against her slick folds, teasing her entrance.

"Please." She arched backward, aching with need. "I need you to fuck me."

Heath growled, his hands gripping her hips as he thrust into her in one smooth stroke. She cried out, her inner walls clenching around him as he filled her completely. This had never been her favorite position before, but something about being on her hands and knees as he pounded into her from behind was thrilling and primal.

Heath's fingers dug into her hips as he drove into her, his cock pulsing with need. "You feel so fucking good," he growled, his hips snapping forward with each thrust. "So tight and wet."

She moaned, her body quivering as he claimed her. "Harder," she begged, her fingers clutching at the sheets as he fucked her. "Don't hold back. You won't hurt the babies."

Heath obliged, his hips slamming against her ass as he pounded into her. "You're mine," he snarled, his voice thick with desire. "My mate."

Maya cried out, her body tensing as she neared her release. "Yes." She gasped, her muscles clenching around his cock as she came. "I'm yours. Only yours."

Heath roared, his cock pulsing as he spilled his seed deep inside her, and she came again, her body trembling with pleasure.

Heath collapsed against her, his chest heaving as he struggled to catch his breath. "You're amazing," he said, his lips brushing against her ear. "I've never felt anything like that before. It was better than the first time and will keep getting better if you accept the mate bond." He kissed her shoulder, trailing his tongue over it. "Here is where I'd bite you."

Maya shuddered, her body aching for more. "I don't understand, but I want you to do it."

Heath shook his head. "Not until you know what it means and what you're agreeing to. I'm not going to force this on you."

Maya frowned. "I'm not afraid."

Heath's eyes flashed with amusement. "You were earlier. I could smell it."

Maya flushed, remembering how she'd fainted. "I was overwhelmed. I didn't know what was happening. I'm sorry."

Heath brushed a strand of hair from her face. "There's nothing to apologize for. I should have explained things to you sooner."

Maya's heart pounded as she once again posed the question that had been weighing on her mind. "Do you really want to be Alpha?" She watched him closely, searching for any hint of his true feelings in the moonlit shadows playing across his face. She traced gentle patterns across his chest as she spoke. "I've noticed how you carry yourself within the pack, the way you interact with everyone. There's a hesitancy, almost like being Alpha isn't where your heart truly lies."

"You're right. Being Alpha has never been my deepest desire. It's a duty I'm expected to assume out of obligation, but it's never felt like my true calling."

"Why continue down that path? Why not consider passing the title to someone who embraces it wholeheartedly, like Tamsin? She's proven herself as Beta, right?"

He nodded. "She possesses the qualities of a natural leader, a strength and determination that commanded respect. The notion of handing over the Alpha mantle to her has crossed my mind before. She has the qualities needed to lead the pack with wisdom and strength."

Maya's fingers paused in their ministrations, her gaze locking onto his as she processed his words. "She seemed willing when we talked to her earlier. If being Alpha isn't your true calling, perhaps it's time to explore other paths."

His heart clenched at the thought, a sudden realization dawning upon him. "Is this your way of telling me to consider a future without you?" he asked, a flicker of uncertainty in his voice. "Are you still having doubts about us?"

"No. It's not about us. In fact, I've come to a decision."

"What is it?" he asked.

"I want to move in with you," she said, keeping her voice steady. "I want to see where this journey takes us, but I'm not ready for marriage just yet."

He looked relieved. "I understand," he said, looping his fingers through hers. "We'll take things one step at a time, at a pace that feels right for both of us." He grinned. "It's a good thing I don't want to be Alpha. Unless I'm mated...married...by my fortieth birthday, I can't Ascend anyway."

"And your birthday is soon?" she asked. When he nodded, she frowned. "You're sure you want to do this? I don't know how we'd make it work with me not living on the island, but I don't want to be the reason you turn your back on your inheritance."

He seemed confident when he said, "You've just given me the impetus to finally decide. I know who and what I want. You."

Chapter Nine

THE EVENING BREEZE carried the scent of burning wood and roasting meats, mingling with the salty tang of the ocean. Heath inhaled deeply, savoring the familiar aromas as he approached the bonfire pit after their lovemaking. Flames danced, casting flickering shadows across the gathered pack members' faces, their expressions a mix of curiosity and anticipation.

Maya's hand rested in the crook of his arm, her fingers lightly gripping his bicep. A subtle squeeze conveyed her silent support, her presence a steadying force as he prepared to address the pack. His gaze swept over the assembled crowd, taking in the familiar faces.

Clearing his throat, he projected his voice, commanding attention without effort. "Thank you all for coming. I know there have been whispers and questions about the future of our pack." His looked pointedly at the elders, whose weathered faces remained etched with disapproval. "It's no secret that I've struggled with the expectations placed upon me."

A murmur rippled through the crowd, heads nodding in acknowledgment. He paused, allowing the weight of his words to settle before continuing. "For too long, I've tried to conform, to be the Alpha you envisioned."

Samson's bushy silver brows were drawn together, while Shaw stared back impassively, his scarred cheek glowing in the firelight. Penson didn't look at him.

Heath gave Maya's hand a gentle, reassuring squeeze as he went on. "That's not who I am. I'm a researcher, driven by curiosity and a thirst for knowledge." He gestured broadly with his free hand. "The city is my domain, not this island."

At this, angry mutters rippled through the crowd. Several voices rose up in dissent before Heath lifted his hand, the simple commanding gesture silencing the protests. "Don't misunderstand. I love the island. It's the heart of our pack, but my heart can't live here all the time. I know this goes against tradition, but traditions can change. The world is evolving, and we must evolve with it."

He turned his gaze to Tamsin, noting the conflicted expression on his cousin's face. Her usual easy confidence was replaced by something more vulnerable.

"That's why I'm stepping down as Alpha," he said, his words dropping like stones into a still pond. "Tamsin has proven herself time and again. She's strong, capable, and understands the needs of our pack better than anyone. She deserves to be Alpha, not limited to Beta—and I mean full Alpha, not restrained by a title like Lupina that will allow others to believe they can make decisions for her." He cast a knowing look at the elders, who grumbled and looked away.

Tamsin's brown eyes widened in surprise, her lips parting slightly as if to speak, though no words came. He offered her a nod of encouragement, hoping to convey his absolute faith in her leadership. This was no snap decision.

"I won't abandon you," Heath assured the stunned crowd, his voice ringing with conviction. "My resources will always be at your disposal, but my path lies elsewhere now, with Maya and our children."

Silence lengthened, the crackling flames the only sound. Then, one by one, pack members began to nod, their expressions shifting from skepticism to acceptance. He was almost giddy with relief as the weight of expectations lifted from his shoulders.

As the night wore on, discussions continued, voices raised in debate and compromise. Heath stood firm, his resolve unshaken, and she stayed by his side. When the last embers from the bonfire snuffed into nothingness the pack had accepted his decision comma and they welcomed Tamsin is their new alpha. He wasn't even slightly disappointed.

THE LOW RUMBLE OF AN outboard motor disrupted the tranquility of the morning. Heath glanced up from where he sat on the sandy shore, scanning the horizon. A small boat came into view, steadily growing larger as it approached the secluded island.

Heath turned to Maya, who was tucked against his side. Her green eyes met his golden ones, a wordless communication passing between the mates. The time had come. After much discussion, they would be leaving the pack behind to start their new life together, just the two of them and their unborn pups.

With a resigned sigh, he rose and pulled her to her feet from the fallen log. Hand in hand, they made their way down the beach, to where the rest of the pack had gathered to see them off.

Tamsin stepped forward, her athletic frame silhouetted against the rising sun. Her mate and their children lingered behind her just slightly. He drew her into a tight embrace, inhaling her familiar woodsy scent one last time.

"Lead them well," he send, his voice thick with emotion.

Tamsin nodded, looking stoic though she appeared to be blinking back tears.

The boat drifted closer through the lapping waves, the engine cutting off as it glided to a stop on the shoreline as Samson returned it close to shore. Heath kept Maya's delicate hand clasped in his larger one as they waded out to the vessel. The water swirled cool and clear around their ankles.

With mingled excitement and melancholy, he helped his pregnant mate over the side of the boat. She settled onto a bench, the sea breeze stirring her dark, wavy hair. Heath's muscular frame flexed as he hopped in beside her.

Samson had already crawled out and stood in the thigh-deep cold water. He sent the elder a nod. The older wolf grumbled at him, but there was a hint of acceptance in his gaze when he clapped Heath on the shoulder. "Hope you don't regret this."

"I won't."

Untethered at last, the boat turned and headed for the open ocean under the power of the outboard motor. Heath slid an arm around Maya's shoulders, holding her close as the island shrank behind them. The rhythmic slap of waves against the hull and cries of gulls overhead accompanied their journey toward the distant horizon and the new chapter awaiting them.

As the island grew smaller in the distance, and the yacht grew closer, he pulled her close, his lips brushing her temple. "A new adventure awaits," he said.

Maya leaned into his embrace. "I can't wait," she send, her hand resting over the swell of her belly, a reminder of the lives they had created, and the future that lay ahead.

As they neared the yacht, Heath allowed himself a moment of reflection. He had defied expectations and found a love that transcended boundaries. He was happy to be just plain Heath again, without the yoke of leadership hanging around his neck. He'd never wanted to be anyone's Alpha, and now I didn't have to be.

Chapter Ten

MAYA SETTLED INTO LIFE with Heath in his spacious penthouse apartment, the city sprawling out before them through the floor-to-ceiling windows. Each morning, she awoke to the aroma of freshly brewed coffee and the sizzle of breakfast cooking in the kitchen. Heath, already dressed for work, always greeted her with a tender kiss and a gentle caress of her growing belly.

As the days turned into weeks, she was falling deeper in love with the man who had unexpectedly become the center of her world. She marveled at his caring support, and the way he anticipated her every need. Whether it was a craving for a specific food, or a desire for a foot massage after a long day, he was always there, ready to provide comfort and care.

One evening as they sat on the balcony, she leaned into his embrace, resting her head on his broad shoulder. The scent of his cologne mingled with the crisp night air, enveloping her in a sense of warmth and security.

"I never thought I would find happiness like this," she said, linking her fingers with his. "You've changed my life in ways I never could have imagined."

His lips brushed against her temple, warming her skin with his breath. "You've changed mine too, Maya. I never knew what it meant to truly love someone until I met you."

As the weeks passed, Maya's belly grew rounder, the twins within her thriving under the love and care she and Heath provided. She was marveling at the changes in her body and the way her skin stretched taut over the life growing inside her.

One morning, as she stood before the mirror, her hands cradling her belly, he appeared behind her, encircling her waist. There was a mischievous glint dancing in his eyes.

"I have a surprise for you," he said, his lips grazing the shell of her ear. "Something I've been planning for a while now."

Her heart fluttered with anticipation as he led her to the rooftop of their building. As they stepped out into the cool morning air, she gasped at the sight before her. A vibrant hot air balloon, its colors a kaleidoscope of reds, oranges, and yellows, waited, tethered to the roof.

"I wanted to propose to you in a way that would take your breath away," he said, his voice soft with emotion. "I had planned to do this in a hot air balloon, high above the city, but the winds are too strong today. I couldn't wait any longer."

He dropped to one knee, a velvet box in his hand. As he opened it, a sparkling diamond ring caught the morning light, its brilliance nearly blinding. "Maya, you've brought joy, love, and purpose to my life. You've given me the greatest gift of all in our children. Will you do me the honor of becoming my wife and mate?"

Tears streamed down Maya's face as she nodded, her voice choked with emotion. "Yes, Heath. Of course, yes."

He slipped the ring onto her finger, the cool metal a perfect fit. He rose to his feet, gathering her in his arms and spinning her around, their laughter echoing across the rooftop.

As they stood there, wrapped in each other's embrace, she glanced at the hot air balloon, a playful smile tugging at her lips. "it's a shame the wind made it impossible to take off. It's OK though. I suppose I'm a hot air balloon myself these days," she joked, patting her rounded belly. "At thirty weeks, I feel like I could float away at any moment."

Heath chuckled, his hand joining hers on her stomach. "You're the most beautiful hot air balloon I've ever seen," he said, his eyes shining with love and adoration.

As they made their way back inside, Maya's heart swelled with the realization that she had found her forever. In Heath's arms, she had discovered a love that would carry them through the challenges and joys of parenthood and beyond.

WHEN THE ALARM CLOCK sounded, Maya stirred, her hand instinctively reaching for is side of the bed, only to find it empty. A faint smile tugged at her lips as the scent of freshly brewed coffee wafted in from the kitchen.

Slipping out from beneath the silken sheets, she padded across the plush carpet, trailing her fingers along the smooth surface of the dresser. She paused, admiring the way the diamond on her engagement ring caught the light, sending shimmering rainbows dancing across the walls.

As she entered the kitchen, the sight that greeted her stole her breath. Heath stood at the stove, his broad shoulders flexing beneath the thin fabric of his T-shirt as he expertly flipped pancakes. The sizzle of butter mingled with the rich aroma of freshly brewed coffee, creating a symphony of scents that made Maya's mouth water.

"Good morning, beautiful," he said with a smile, his hazel eyes crinkling at the corners.

She crossed the kitchen, her arms encircling his waist from behind. She nuzzled her cheek against the firm planes of his back, reveling in the warmth of his body, and the steady rhythm of his heartbeat. "Mmm, something smells delicious," she said, her lips brushing against the nape of his neck.

He chuckled, the rumble of his laughter vibrating through her. "I'm trying a new recipe for blueberry pancakes. Thought you might enjoy a little indulgence this morning."

Maya's eyes widened as she caught sight of the stack of fluffy pancakes, studded with plump, juicy blueberries. "You spoil me, Mr. Garrison."

"Only the best for my fiancée and our little ones," he said, his free hand coming to rest on the swell of her belly as he turned to face her, the plate of pancakes in his left hand.

They settled at the table. As Maya savored each bite of the delectable pancakes, she said, "I've been thinking about the wedding."

He paused, his fork hovering in midair, his gaze fixed on her with rapt attention.

"I know we had discussed having the ceremony soon, but I think it might be best to postpone it until after your birthday."

A flicker of concern passed over Heath's features, and he reached across the table, his fingers intertwining with hers. "Is everything all right, Maya? If you're having second thoughts, I understand. We can take all the time you need."

Maya shook her head, a gentle smile playing on her lips. "No, no second thoughts. It's just... well, I've been thinking about Tamsin and the pack."

Heath's brow furrowed, and he leaned back in his chair, his thumb absently tracing circles over the back of her hand.

"I know how important tradition is to them, and I wouldn't want our wedding to complicate matters. Tamsin is still adjusting to her role as Alpha, and I don't want to add any unnecessary stress or tension."

A soft sigh escaped Heath's lips, and he nodded, his expression one of understanding. "You're right. Tamsin has been shouldering a lot of responsibility, and the last thing I want is for our happiness to cause her any additional strain or give anyone an excuse to try to push me to take over if I get married before my birthday."

Maya's heart swelled with love and appreciation for the man before her. His willingness to put the needs of his pack first, even at the temporary cost of their own joy, spoke volumes about his character.

"I love you for considering her, Maya. Tamsin might not show it, but she respects you deeply."

A weight lifted from her shoulders, and she leaned across the table, pressing a tender kiss to Heath's lips. "Thank you for understanding, my love. Our wedding will be even more special when the time is right."

ON THE MORNING OF HIS birthday, Maya awoke before the first rays of dawn, carefully slipping out of bed so as not to disturb Heath's slumber. She made her way to the kitchen, her heart fluttering with excitement as she prepared a special breakfast spread, complete with his favorite dishes and a decadent chocolate cake adorned with candles.

As the sun began to peek over the horizon, she returned to the bedroom, a tray laden with the birthday feast balanced in her hands. She set it down on the nightstand, her lips curving into a tender smile as she gazed upon his peaceful form.

Leaning down, she brushed a featherlight kiss against his forehead, her fingers trailing through the soft strands of his hair.

"Happy birthday, my love," she whispered, her voice thick with emotion.

Heath stirred, his eyes fluttering open, and in that moment, Maya said, "Get up and get dressed. We have a flight to catch."

THE ISLAND WHERE THEY'D celebrated his fortieth anniversary faded into the distance as the yacht ferried them back to the airstrip. They soon boarded the private jet and soared through the cloudless sky back toward the glittering skyline of New York City. Her gaze lingered on the azure expanse of the ocean below, mind awash with memories of the past few days spent celebrating Heath's birthday amidst the lush, tropical paradise.

She looked up when he called her name. His hazel eyes met hers, a mischievous glint dancing within their depths. "What do you say we make a little detour?"

Maya arched an inquisitive brow, her lips curving into a playful smile. "A detour? Where did you have in mind?"

He leaned closer, his breath tantalizingly warm against her ear. "Vegas."

A thrill of excitement coursed through her as the implications of his suggestion sank in. Vegas—the city of neon lights, indulgence, quickie marriages, and spontaneity. A place where dreams could come true in the blink of an eye.

"Are you suggesting what I think you're suggesting?" she asked.

Heath's response was a wordless nod, his eyes sparkling with a mixture of love and mischief.

Without a moment's hesitation, she turned to the pilot and raised her voice so he could hear her in the cockpit, which wasn't enclosed. "Change of plans, Captain. Set a course for Las Vegas."

As the jet banked sharply, altering its trajectory, exhilaration hit her. She was embarking on a new adventure, one that would bind her to Heath for the rest of their lives.

The hours seemed to blur together as the jet soared across the country, each minute bringing them closer to their destination. Maya's heart raced with anticipation, her fingers absently toying with the diamond solitaire that adorned her left hand.

Finally, the neon-drenched skyline of Las Vegas came into view, a kaleidoscope of colors and lights that danced across the inky blackness of the night sky. As the jet touched down, giddy excitement bubbled within her.

They wasted no time, Heath's hand firmly clasped in hers as they made their way through the hotel lobby a while later. Maya's senses were heightened, and every sight, sound, and smell seemed more vibrant.

Not even an hour later, she gazed up at the charming little chapel, its stained glass windows spilling colorful light onto the sidewalk. She took in the intricately carved wooden doors and rough-hewn stone facade, picturing herself walking down the aisle inside.

Heath paused and turned to face her. Though he said nothing, his unspoken question hung in the air between them. Was she truly ready for this? Maya's answer came in the form of a radiant smile, her eyes crinkling at the corners. She gave a small, certain nod.

Taking her hand, Heath led her up the steps and through the heavy doors into the hushed interior. Maya blinked, her eyes adjusting to the dim lighting within. Sunbeams filtering through the stained glass dappled the worn wooden pews in a kaleidoscope of jewel tones. The musty, comforting scent of incense enveloped her.

Maya's heart raced as she stood before Heath, the flickering candlelight casting a warm glow over his chiseled features. His golden eyes shone with a depth of emotion that threatened to steal her breath. She could scarcely believe they had made it to this moment after all the twists and turns their journey had taken.

The officiant cleared his throat, his gentle voice breaking the reverent silence that had fallen over the chapel. "Heath Garrison, do you take Maya Holt to be your lawfully wedded wife, to have and to hold, in sickness and in health, for richer or poorer, until death do you part?"

Heath's gaze never wavered from Maya's as he spoke, his voice rich and unwavering. "I do." The simple words carried a weight that resonated deep within Maya's soul.

The officiant turned to Maya, his eyes twinkling with kindness. "Maya Holt, do you take Heath Garrison to be your lawfully wedded husband, to have and to hold, in sickness and in health, for richer or poorer, until death do you part?"

Maya's lips curved into a smile, her heart swelling with a love so profound, it threatened to overwhelm her. "I do," she whispered, her voice thick with emotion.

As they exchanged rings, the cool metal a tangible symbol of their eternal bond, she marveled at the journey that had brought them to this moment. She remembered the first time she had laid eyes on the CEO version of Heath, his presence commanding the room with an intensity that had left her breathless. Little had she known then that this enigmatic man would become the center of her world, the missing piece she hadn't even missed until it was found.

His fingers brushed against hers in a gentle caress that sent shivers racing down her spine. His touch was electric, igniting a fire within her that burned brighter with each passing moment. She gazed up at him, her eyes shining with love and adoration, and saw her own emotions reflected in the depths of his golden irises.

The officiant's voice broke through Maya's reverie, his words ringing with a sense of finality. "By the power vested in me, I now pronounce you husband and wife. You may kiss the bride."

Time seemed to slow as Heath cupped Maya's face in his hands, his touch reverent. Slowly, he leaned in, his lips capturing hers in a kiss that set here soul ablaze. It was a kiss that spoke of promises kept, of dreams realized, and of a love that knew no bounds. Maya melted into Heath's embrace, her fingers tangling in the soft strands of his hair as she surrendered herself to the overwhelming tide of emotions that threatened to sweep her away.

When at last they parted, breathless and flushed, she was lost in the depths of Heath's gaze once more. No words were needed in that moment, for their hearts beat as one, their souls intertwined in a bond that transcended the physical realm.

"My wife," he said, the words sending a delicious shiver down her spine. "My beautiful, incredible wife."

Maya tilted her head back, her eyes meeting Heath's in a silent exchange that spoke volumes. She traced the contours of his face with trembling fingers, committing everything to memory.

"My husband," she whispered, her voice thick with emotion. "My love, my life, my everything."

They emerged from the chapel several minutes later aglow with the radiance of newlyweds. The neon lights of the city seemed to pulse in time with the rapid beating of Maya's heart. Their hotel suite located in the same hotel as the chapel, was a luxurious oasis where they could revel in the depths of their love without restraint. As the door clicked shut behind them, Maya was enveloped in Heath's embrace, his lips claiming hers in a searing kiss that ignited every nerve ending in her body.

The opulent suite enveloped them in a cocoon of luxury, the scent of roses and vanilla permeating the air. Heath led Maya to the king-sized bed, their fingers intertwined, hearts pounding in sync. The city lights twinkled beyond the floor-to-ceiling windows, casting a warm glow on their faces.

Heath's hazel eyes smoldered with desire, his muscular frame taut with restrained passion. He cupped her face, his thumb tracing the curve of her cheek. "Maya," he whispered, his voice husky with emotion, "My mate, my wife."

She leaned into his touch, her breath hitching as his lips brushed against hers. The kiss deepened, their tongues dancing in a sensual rhythm that left them her breathless. Heath's hands roamed her body, exploring every curve and contour with reverence. She tangled her fingers in his hair, pulling him closer as she surrendered to the intoxicating desire coursing through her veins.

He trailed kisses down her neck, grazing his teeth against her sensitive skin. She gasped, trembling with pleasure. He unzipped the dress she'd bought at the store adjacent to the chapel. The fabric pooling at her feet left her clad in only her lacy lingerie. Heath's gaze devoured her, his eyes darkening with lust. "You're so beautiful," he said, his voice thick with desire.

She reached for the buttons of his shirt, her fingers fumbling in her eagerness. He chuckled, his laughter low and seductive, as he helped her undress him. His shirt fell to the floor, revealing his tanned, muscular chest. Maya ran her fingers over his defined abs, marveling at the feel of his smooth, warm skin.

Heath guided her to the bed, his lips never leaving hers. They tumbled onto the soft sheets, their limbs entwined as they lost themselves in their passionate embrace. His fingers traced the lace of her bra, teasing her sensitive nipples through the fabric.

He deftly unhooked Maya's bra, freeing her swollen breasts before he lowered his head, taking a taut nipple into his mouth. She arched her back, a moan escaping her lips as he lavished attention on her sensitive flesh. His tongue swirled and teased, eliciting gasps of pleasure from Maya.

He explored her body with reverence, hooking his fingers into the waistband of her panties to slide them down her legs. She kicked them off, her body trembling with anticipation as he gazed at her, eyes filled with desire and love. "Maya," he whispered, his voice thick with emotion. "You're mine."

Maya reached for him, tracing the waistband of his boxers. Heath helped her remove them, his arousal springing free. She wrapped her hand around his hard length, her thumb tracing the bead of moisture at the tip. Heath groaned, his hips bucking involuntarily.

He gently pushed Maya onto her back, trailing kisses down her stomach. He reached the apex of her thighs, his breath hot against her sensitive flesh. Maya's heart raced as Heath parted her folds, his tongue darting out to taste her pussy. She cried out, writhing with pleasure as he explored her intimately.

Heath's tongue flicked and teased, driving Maya to the brink of ecstasy. She clutched the sheets, trembling as waves of pleasure washed over her. His fingers joined his tongue, teasing her sensitive nub as he delved deeper. Her moans filled the room as she surrendered to the exquisite torment.

He increased his pace, his tongue and fingers working in tandem to send her soaring. She tensed, her muscles coiling as she teetered on the edge. With a final flick of his tongue, he sent her crashing over the precipice. Maya cried out, convulsing as she rode the waves of her orgasm.

As she recovered, he kissed his way up her body, his lips finding hers in a passionate kiss. She could taste herself on his tongue, the intimacy of the act sending a fresh wave of desire coursing through her.

Heath positioned himself behind Maya, his hands caressing her hips as he guided her onto all fours. The classic doggy-style position, traditional for a wolf-shifter, felt natural and right. Maya's heart raced with anticipation.

His fingers traced the curve of Maya's spine, sending shivers throughout her body. He leaned forward, brushing his lips against her ear. "Are you ready, my love?" he asked, his voice husky with desire.

Maya nodded, her breath hitching as she whispered, "Yes, I'm ready."

Heath's fingers found her slick entrance, teasing her with slow, deliberate strokes. Maya moaned, rocking her hips back to meet his touch. With a low growl, he positioned himself at her entrance and then pushed forward, his hard cock sliding into her welcoming heat. She gasped, her body stretching to accommodate him. Heath stilled, allowing her to adjust to his size.

She trembled as his fingers intertwined with hers, their hands pressed against the soft sheets. He began to move, his thrusts slow and deliberate. Her moans soon filled the room.

Heath's fingers tightened around Maya's, his breathing becoming ragged. As their rhythm increased, he leaned forward, his lips finding the sensitive spot on Maya's shoulder. She shivered and his lips skimmed the spot where he'd leave his mark. She trembled with desire when has teeth grazed her skin, his wolf urging him to mark her as his own.

Heath's teeth grazed Maya's shoulder, the sensitive spot where their mating mark would be etched forever. With a low growl, he sank his teeth into her shoulder. The sensation was unlike anything she had ever experienced before. It was as if a jolt of electricity shot through her, igniting every nerve ending in her body. She could feel their connection deepening, their souls meshing in a way that transcended the physical.

She cried out, her body convulsing as she reached her peak. As his teeth sank deeper into her shoulder, she could feel the mating mark taking shape. It was a symbol of their love, their commitment to each other, and their bond as mates. He could feel the power of the mark coursing through him, filling him with a sense of peace and contentment he had never known before.

Maya's cries of pleasure grew louder, writhing beneath him as she surrendered to the intensity of their connection. With one final thrust, Heath reached his own climax. The mating mark pulsed with energy, the power of their connection surging through her as he came inside her. She trembled, her muscles clenching around him as she joined him in ecstasy once more.

As their breathing slowed and their hearts returned to a normal rhythm, Heath gently withdrew his teeth from Maya's shoulder. The mating mark throbbed pleasantly beneath his lips, a constant reminder of their love and commitment to each other.

As they lay there, wrapped in each other's arms, She had never been happier. She traced the mating mark on her shoulder, a soft smile playing on her lips. "I love you, Heath," she whispered, her voice filled with emotion.

"I love you too, Maya," he Said, his voice husky with emotion. "Forever and always."

As they drifted off to sleep, wrapped in each other's arms, she was certain their love would endure. They were mates, bound together by an unbreakable bond, and nothing could ever tear them apart.

Epilogue

THE CONTRACTIONS INTENSIFIED, each wave of pain more powerful than the last. Maya gripped the edge of the hospital bed, her knuckles whitening as she fought through the searing agony. Beads of sweat glistened on her brow, and her chest heaved with labored breaths.

Heath was by her side, his strong hand enveloping hers. His hazel eyes shone with a mixture of concern and support. "You're doing great, Maya. Just breathe through it." His deep voice rumbled, laced with a soothing timbre that momentarily eased her discomfort.

The midwife, a kindly woman with graying hair and a reassuring presence, monitored Maya's progress. "The babies are ready to meet their parents. On the next contraction, I need you to push with all your might."

Maya nodded, steeling herself for the monumental task ahead. As the next wave of pain crested, she bore down. Heath's arm encircled her shoulders, lending his strength.

"That's it, love. You're doing beautifully," he said, brushing his lips against her damp forehead.

Minutes ticked by, each one an eternity of exertion and determination. Maya's cries mingled with the encouragement of the midwife and Heath's steadfast support. Finally, after what seemed like an endless battle, the first piercing wail of new life filled the room.

"It's a boy," said the midwife, cradling the squirming bundle in her arms.

Tears of joy streamed down Maya's cheeks as she caught a glimpse of her son, his tiny face scrunched up in protest at the sudden change in his world. Heath's eyes glistened with pride and wonder, his gaze transfixed on the miracle they had created together.

Before she could fully revel in the moment, another contraction gripped her, signaling the arrival of their second child. With a renewed surge of energy, she pushed, her body straining to bring forth the next precious life.

"One more, Maya. You can do it," he said, his voice a steady mantra in her ear.

With a final, earth-shattering effort, a second cry pierced the air, announcing the arrival of their daughter. The midwife expertly swaddled the newborn, presenting her to the awestruck parents.

Maya's heart swelled with an indescribable love as she cradled her son in her arms, his tiny fist curled around her finger. Heath gazed down at their daughter, his expression filled with joy, wonder, and a hint of protectiveness.

"They're perfect," she whispered in a voice thick with emotion.

Heath leaned down, pressing a tender kiss to her forehead. "Just like their mother."

The world seemed to fade away, leaving only the four of them cocooned in a bubble of pure bliss. Maya studied the delicate features of her son, marveling at the perfection of his tiny nose and rosebud lips. Heath gently traced a finger along their daughter's cheek, his touch featherlight and reverent.

The midwife discreetly slipped from the room, granting the new family a moment of privacy to bask in the wonder of their creation.

"We still haven't decided what to name them. Any ideas?" asked Maya, her gaze flickering between the two bundles of joy.

He smiled down at them. "I was thinking Easton for our son, and Janie for our little princess."

She gave him a tired but blissful smile. "Easton and Janie. I love it."

They sat in comfortable silence, drinking in the sight of their newborns, their hearts overflowing with a love so profound, it threatened to consume them. Maya marveled at the tiny miracles they had brought into the world, their perfect blend of human and wolf-shifter heritage.

As she gazed upon Easton and Janie's peaceful faces, she was thankful for everything that had led to this moment. From the initial shock of discovering she'd received the wrong sperm to the revelation of Heath's true nature, every step had been worth it to bring them here.

His arm tightened around her shoulders, and she leaned into his comforting embrace, their children nestled between them. In that sacred space, they were a family ready to embark on the greatest adventure of their lives.

About The Author

AURELIA SKYE IS THE pen name *USA Today* bestselling author Kit Tunstall uses when writing science fiction and paranormal romance. It's simply a way to separate the myriad types of stories she writes so readers know what to expect with each "author."

Kit's Website[1]

1. https://kittunstall.com/

Also by Aurelia Skye

Alien Baby Pact
Baby For The Brundle Commander
Baby For The Serp General
Alien Baby Pact Compilation
Baby For The Grimlock General
Baby For The Palantir Chief
Baby For The Alphan Captain
Baby For The Mosaic Med Chief
Baby For The Tark Commander

Alien Baby Pakt
Alien Baby Pakt Zusammenstellung

Celestial Mates
Wrong Place, Right Mate
Destined For The Drakari Warlords

Cybernetic Hearts

Mated To The Cyborg General
Claimed By The Cyborg Commander
Fated For The Cyborg Officer
Meant For The Cyborg Captain
Baby For The Cyborg General
Cybernetic Hearts: Complete Series

Dazon Agenda
Written In The Stars
Alien's Babies
Diplomatic Affairs
Moon Madness
Across The Stars
Emperor's Assassin Bride
Dazon Agenda: Complete Collection

Future Fairytales
Hooked

Guerriers Blessés
Chassé
Inlassable
Marqué
Justice
Compilation Guerriers Blessés

Harrow Bay
Hell Gates & Hot Flashes
Nightmares & Night Sweats
Warlocks & Wrinkles
Love Spells & Liver Spots
Phantasms & Presbyopia
Vampires & Varicose Veins
Mermaids & Mood Swings
Séances & Sagging Skin
Necromancy & Knee Pains
Marids & Memory Loss
Devil Deals & Dizzy Spells
Happy Endings & New Beginnings
Harrow Bay, Volume 1
Hellhounds & Mistletoe
Harrow Bay, Volume 2
Harrow Bay, Volume 3
Harrow Bay Complete Series

Harrow Bucht Serie
Höllentore & Hitzewallungen
Alpträume Und Nachtschweiß
Hexenmeister & Falten
Liebeszauber Und Leberflecken
Phantasmen Und Alterssichtigkeit
Vampire und Krampfadern
Meerjungfrauen Und Stimmungsschwankungen
Séancen Und Schlaffe Haut
Nekromantie Und Knieschmerzen

Marids und Gedächtnisverlust
Teufelsgeschäfte Und Schwindelzauber
Happy Ends Und Neuanfängen
Höllenhunde & Mistelzweige

Hell Virus
Catching Hell
Surviving Hell
Bleeding Hell
Raising Hell
Sharing Hell

Howls Romance
The Jaguar Alpha's Forbidden Lover
CEO Wolf Shifter's Surprise Twins

Northstar Shifters
Northstar Heir's Scarred Mate

Olympus Station
Station Commander's Surrogate
Alien Prince's Secret Baby
Security Agent's Alien Bartender
Olympus Station Compilation

SpicyShorts
Music In My Heart
Kilted Tentacle Monster: A Search for True Love

Sweet Escapes
Hook & Wendy

The Haunting of Clara Gray
Ghostly Awakening

Three Crones Inn
Vastly Inn-proved
Ghastly Intentions
Grave Inn-tervention
Ghostly Inn-heritance
Three Crones Inn Compilation

True North
True North #1: Death & Deception
True North #2: Rescued & Revelations
True North #3: Fire & Ice
True North #4: Enemies & Lovers
True North #5: Truth & Tiranog
True North #6: Fight & Flight

True North #7: Love & Loss

Wounded Warriors
Relentless
Marked
Justice
Wounded Warriors Collection
Hunted

Standalone
Reluctant Companion
Princess By Mistake
Fire Lord's Assistant
True North
Dragon Laird's Witch
Alien General's Rebel Consort
Tempted By Demons
Enemy Combatant
Grotesquerie
Mistaken Bounty
Wahre Richtung
Power Surges & Amorous Urges
Taken By The Orc General
Compilation Alien Baby Pact

Also by Kit Tunstall

After The End
Unraveling
Unyielding

Howls Romance
CEO Wolf Shifter's Surprise Twins

TnT Storybuilders
Building Your World: A Guide For Writers
Action Thriller Storybuilder: A Guide For Writers
Instant Love Novelette Storybuilder
Instant Love Novella Storybuilder: A Guide For Writers
Contemporary Reverse Harem Novel Storybuilder
Contemporary Romance Novel Storybuilder
Cozy Mystery Novel Storybuilder
Dark Romance Storybuilder
Gothic Romance Storybuilder
Ménage Novelette Storybuilder
Ménage Novella Storybuilder
Ménage Novel Storybuilder

Paranormal Revere Harem Storybuilder
Paranormal Romance Novel Storybuilder
Psychological Thriller Storybuilder
Regency Romance Storybuilder
Science Fiction Romance Novella Storybuilder
Spicy Novella Storybuilder
Sweet Novella Storybuilder
Romantic Suspense Storybuilder: A Guide For Writers

Standalone
Holiday Tales: Four Short Stories of Thanksgiving and Christmas
Master's Gift
Dragon Laird's Witch
Baby Daddies: Older Men & Babies Collection
Christmas Kiss: Limited Edition Six-Story Holiday Collection
Sampler: SF, Contemporary & Historical Collection

Watch for more at www.kittunstall.com.